I0534747

Holiday Bliss
A Penning Valley Christmas Anthology

This is a work of fiction. Similarities to real people, places, or events are entirely coincidental.

HOLIDAY BLISS

First edition. December 19, 2023.

Copyright © 2023 K. McCoy et al..

ISBN: 979-8991737630

Written by K. McCoy et al..

Table of Contents

Copyright

Foreword

These days it's almost too easy to forget the reason for the season. With our busy schedules, pursuing our dreams, and spending time away from our loved ones, the heart of the season can take some time to find. It is with this thought in mind that we present to you all Holiday Bliss. Each story is uniquely different, but at their core, they each will remind you that love is at the helm of all things. Like a bright star on top of the highest Christmas tree, let this holiday anthology sweep you away and leave behind all the warm and (oh so spicy!) fuzzies.

And on that note, please enjoy reading Holiday Bliss!

• • ❧ • •

-K. McCoy

1

'Twas Two Weeks Til...

by ShaRhonda Sharp

When the lines of "professional" blur into "personal," the lights may not be the only thing tangled in the tinsel.

Leticia "Tecie" Nadal loves where she is in life and the only season better than the "Growth" one she's in, is the holiday season. It's the busiest time of year for her, but she loves every minute of it...as long as everything is going exactly how she planned, of course. However, when Leticia gets blindsided by one of her contractors quitting without any notice and just two weeks before the biggest event of her career, she's certain this is as bad as it can get...until the "Replacement" shows up.

Dominic "Domino" Ballantyne has a reputation he's been striving to outgrow since graduating high school and realizing his desired happiness required him to change. The process of growing up from a problematic teenager into a responsible businessman has not been easy, and the constant run-ins with people from his past reminding him of who and how he used to be, do not help. But when he lays eyes on Leticia Nadal again after more than a decade, he gladly welcomes the reminder of how he's always felt about her, his "Tecie Baby." Dominic has never been more grateful for inheriting someone else's messy workload than he was when he realized she was the client he's working for. Now with two weeks to work in such close contact with Leticia, Dominic has some plans of his own to add to her checklist.

Chapter 1

'Twas two weeks til'...

.. ∞ ..

The chimes of the elevator ascending one floor after another inside Willis Tower, blended with the early morning chatter of fellow office arrivers, surrounded Leticia Nadal as she crammed in for her thirty-four-floor ride. She was mentally rattling off her checklist for what needed to be done today as she periodically shifted her stance to allow passengers on and off at their respective floors. It was Monday, which officially put her at the two-week mark before the Mayor's Christmas Masquerade Party.

The Mayor's Director of Community Affairs, who also happened to be her brother-in-law, Hector, personally commissioned Leticia to coordinate an extravagant, yet charitable, affair. She excitedly accepted the project back in October, but now with her deadline creeping closer and closer, that "Grinch" known as stress and anxiety she had been able to ignore before was finally digging its nails in.

The flashing green numbers entranced Leticia as she continued mumbling the to-do list to herself. The doors parted at her floor, and she was met with the immediate bombardment of morning greetings and holiday radio blaring from the overhead speakers. Leticia smiled and waved politely, like she did every morning, as she continued the trek to her courtesy office.

The Director of Building Operations had provided Leticia a stationary workspace for the last six weeks leading up to the event to help make her life easier in overseeing the site and her team, of which

5

she was extremely grateful. She noticed the door was already propped open, indicating her assistant, De'Vyne, had beat her into the office.

"Good morning, gorgeous!" Leticia sang as she entered the office.

"Good morning, Boss Lady! Happy Monday!" De'Vyne greeted in Spanish with a huge grin across his face.

"Oh! Well, happy Monday to you, too!" she responded back in Spanish with a proud smile. "How was your weekend?"

"It was great, despite the snow. Not that it stopped me," he continued with a wink.

"Ooh! Look at you! I see them Babbel courses have been paying off, huh?"

"You see me?!"

Leticia bursts into joyous giggles as she high fived her assistant. When De'Vyne first started working for her, he said since she was half Dominican, he wanted to learn Spanish to speak to Leticia in her other native language sometimes.

"Gotta give you a taste of home after code-switching all day, ya know?" he would often say.

De'Vyne was a beautiful, brown skinned, bearded, meticulously well-kempt, mildly flamboyant Black man with the most exquisite makeup skills Leticia had ever seen. He had joined her team about six months ago, and she was so glad, too; because when the mayor's office came calling, he was the loudest voice cheering her on and jumping in to help at every moment, even without her having to ask. There was nothing he wouldn't do to ensure she succeeded at the biggest event of her career.

"Here is your calendar, presentation deck and favorite purple clipboard with today's checklist," De'Vyne presented the items stacked neatly on the corner of his desk.

"Ugh! Bless you!" Leticia sighed heavily as she slipped out of her coat and hung it up.

"Okay, outfit!" he praised, snapping his fingers.

Leticia wore a long red and black checkered tweed blazer over a cream-colored flowy jumpsuit and red pumps. A long silver necklace with multicolored stones hung down to her diaphragm and matching earrings dangled from her ears. Her long, dark curly hair was pulled back into a wavy ponytail, and she donned her favorite burgundy lipstick that unlocked her "Baddie" attitude every time. Leticia spun around, showing off every angle and posing like a runway model as she laughed giddily.

She blew De'Vyne a kiss when he handed over her Christmas-themed thermos filled with piping hot peppermint mocha fresh from the Keurig behind him. She asked if he'd been upstairs to walk the event site yet, because she was anxious to know what progress had been made by the decorators. He said he hadn't but would run up while she was in her meeting with Hector and his team giving them status updates on everything.

"And yes, I will take pictures and send them to you," De'Vyne confirmed with a wide grin, batting his medium mink eyelashes.

"And video!" Leticia quipped, pointing a rose gold stiletto fingernail his way.

"Yes, ma'am!" he replied with a laugh.

"Have you seen Emilio today?" she asked about the sound and lighting engineer they were working with.

"I haven't, actually."

"He hasn't answered any of my calls or texts the last couple days either."

De'Vyne assured her he'd track down Emilio when he went upstairs and bring her a full report of everything as he headed out. Leticia gathered her meeting materials, cellphone and coffee and prepared to leave, as well. Before walking out, she stopped at the full-length mirror hanging behind the door. After assessing her reflection and being satisfied with what she saw, Leticia looked herself in the eyes and gave a quick pep talk.

"You are fucking dope! You are the bomb! You deserve to be here! You are the best person for the job and every-fucking-body knows it! If they don't, they will! You're Leticia Nadal, dammit!"

Leticia gave a confident nod and smile to her reflection then marched out of her office and down the hall to the conference room, strutting just as boldly as she felt.

"What the hell is this?!" Leticia barked in a high voice as she entered the open event space.

De'Vyne had sent photos as promised, and what she saw made it nearly impossible to keep her composure during her meeting. The team of contracted decorators were in the process of hanging giant ornaments from the ceiling and wrapping the banisters and balconies in tinsel and strings of lights when Leticia walked in. The problem was the entire color scheme they had going was all off and nothing close to what she originally instructed them to do.

"Boss Lady, it's okay. I got it," De'Vyne tried to reassure her.

"Dev, what the hell?! How the hell?!" Leticia exclaimed each question as she swept her arms through the air in confusion.

"I have no idea, but I'll take care of it," he promised.

"We are down to the wire here. We ain't got time for this mess!"

"I know. I know. I'll handle it. You got enough to deal with. Let me get this."

Leticia begrudgingly conceded and demanded this issue be resolved by Wednesday at the latest because they had a very tight schedule to keep.

De'Vyne nodded his understanding and made his way over to the huddle of contractors, gruffly barking orders as he went. She called after him, asking if he'd run into Emilio yet, and he said he still hadn't seen him.

"Where the hell is he?" Leticia mumbled to herself as she pulled her cellphone out to call him again.

This time it went straight to voicemail and a small twinge of panic set in until she turned the corner and saw a man inside the electrical closet with his back to the door. She released a sigh of relief and quickly began rattling off her list of expectations.

"Good morning, Emilio," Leticia said, trying to mask her annoyance and looking down at her clipboard. "Hope you're ready to work today, because we have a lot to do. First thing's first, we need to do a walkthrough to make sure all the sockets are operable and make a final decision on where the cords will run."

Leticia continued robotically naming things on her checklist and asking for updates on certain items, but stopped when she realized Emilio still hadn't said a word.

"Emilio, you haven't answered any of my questions," Leticia said, dropping her pseudo-pleasant tone.

"Probably because Emilio ain't here," the man said sarcastically, finally turning to face her.

"Domino," she exhaled in a breathy whisper of surprise.

The coverall-clad man with his hat turned backwards narrowed his gaze in suspicion as he looked at Leticia. He tilted his head to the left and twisted his mouth as if in deep thought and contemplation. Who was this woman calling him by such a familiar name only reserved for those closest to him.

"I know you?" he asked in a gravelly voice.

"Yeah...I mean, you used to," Leticia replied nervously. "We went to Jefferson High together. It's Leticia."

"Tecie?!" he asked in a shocked tone, his eyes wide.

"Oh, wow. Haven't heard that name in years."

"Yeah, neither have I."

Dominic "Domino" Ballantyne lowered his lids, taking his gaze from shocked to intrigued. He drank in the sight of the woman standing in front him, letting his eyes roam over her face as if committing it to memory. Not that he had ever forgotten it, even after all these years. She mostly looked the same, but there was a certain mature edginess about her now that he was immediately drawn to like a moth to a flame.

He emerged from the electrical closet, making Leticia take several steps backwards, as she tried to regulate her nervous breathing. Of all the people in Chicago — in the world — Domino Ballantyne was the absolute last person she'd ever expected to run into. It had been over ten years since she'd last seen him, and she still practically drooled at the sight of him.

Dominic had the most gorgeous golden-brown complexion that was practically flawless, except for a light patch of skin forming a birthmark around his left eye. A shadowy beard covered his strong jaw and encircled blush pink lips; and full thick eyebrows hovered above deep brown eyes. Even though his jumpsuit looked oversized, Leticia could vividly see the broad expanse of his chest and shoulders, and quietly wondered what other secrets his uniform was hiding.

The feel of Dominic's hand cupping her elbow made Leticia snap out of her trance. She blinked slowly as the entirety of his face came back into view and she remembered where she was and what she was doing.

"You good?" Dominic asked softly.

"Huh? Yeah, I'm good," Leticia replied, her words coming out faster than normal. "Uh, wh-what are you doing here?"

"That's what I'm trying to figure out, actually," he said, his mouth twisting up again.

"Where is Emilio? He hasn't responded to any of my calls or texts, and I need him here ASAP."

"Yeah, he ain't responding to anybody. As luck would have it, Emilio got himself a winning lottery ticket last week and disappeared without a word."

"What?!"

Chapter 2
'Twas still two weeks til...

· · ⚜ · ·

Dominic informed Leticia that Emilio had skipped town without a word or warning, leaving him to inherit a bulk of the workload left behind. The problem was that all of Emilio's projects were "in progress" and there was no way of finding out what had already been done, what else needed to be done or what the final results were supposed to be without asking the client. Something Dominic hated doing because he always felt it made him look incompetent. This time was no different.

"I'm trying to figure out what the hell was he doing so I know what I need to do, but it's looking easier said than done," Dominic said as he huffed in frustration and shoved his hands in the pockets of his jumpsuit.

"This can't be happening!" Leticia exclaimed, no longer able to withhold her panic.

"It's not as bad as it looks," he replied, trying hard to sound convincing.

"No, you don't understand," she said frantically. "This is the biggest event of my career. I can't not pull this off, and the last thing I need is people going M.I.A. Especially now!"

Leticia slammed her clipboard and cellphone down on a nearby table and began pacing back and further, murmuring, and cursing in Spanish as she went. First the decor fiasco and now this! What the hell else could possibly go wrong?! she thought to herself. Her heels

11

collided angrily with the floor tiles as she exhaled one heavy breath after another between grumbles and murmurs.

Leticia stopped pacing long enough to reign herself in by remembering the mantra she said in the mirror mere hours ago. Taking a deep breath and releasing it slowly, she turned on her heels to face Dominic, who was now standing directly behind her. He caught her by the waist, barely stopping them from crashing into each other, and her hands landed on his chest. Their eyes met and for a moment everything around them faded to black.

His strong hands gripped her sides, sinking his fingertips into the softness of her flesh beneath the thin fabric of her jumpsuit. Leticia's fingers flexed against the material of Dominic's coveralls, feeling the firmness of his chest and steadiness of his heartbeat underneath. His eyes dropped to her mouth when he saw the tip of her tongue dart out and swipe across her parted lips, making him swallow hard.

"It's okay," Dominic said softly, blinking slowly and bringing his eyes back to hers. "Short notice and tight deadlines are my specialty. I got you. I promise."

"Okay," Leticia whispered as a slight smile formed on her lips.

Dominic gave a comforting wink before taking a step back, letting his fingers drag along Leticia's curves as he released the hold he had on her. Her breath shuddered in her throat at the sensation of his hands grazing her body, and she instantly felt an emptiness when he was no longer touching her.

"So," Dominic started as he put his now empty hands back into his pockets. "I just need a little time to figure out where Emilio left off, and I can take it from there."

"Oh, um…I can help with that," Leticia chimed in after regaining her composure. "If you remember, I was the one who always took notes and wrote down everything."

Leticia went over to the table where she'd slammed down her things and rifled through the pile, retrieving a legal pad and the presentation deck from her meeting earlier. She flipped through the pages of the legal pad until she found her notes from all the previous walkthroughs with Emilio and ripped out the pages.

"These are very detailed but easy to follow, I promise," Leticia explained with a soft chuckle. "And there are photos of everything in this PowerPoint to give you a visual. I hope this helps."

"Tecie Nadal saving my life, once again," Dominic said with a smirk as he flipped through the pages.

"If you're as good as you say, then you'll be saving my life too."

"I am."

Leticia turned her head to hide the smile and redness flushing across her face. She gathered her things and told Dominic she'd leave him alone to get to work.

"My, uh, number is, uh, on the first page of that presentation," Leticia informed him as she started backing away to leave. "If you need anything, just call or text me. I'm pretty much attached to this phone now."

"I'll definitely call you," Dominic said, his deep, raspy voice smothering each word in a sensuality he didn't even bother to hide.

Leticia was so stunned by his definite tone and the flirty glint in his eyes that she lost all ability to speak, and just settled for an awkward wave as she rushed to walk away. She was walking so fast, she almost crashed into De'Vyne, who was watching her like a hawk.

"Oh, hey. Did you get the decorators sorted out?" Leticia asked, trying to sound professional.

"Yeah, I did," De'Vyne said dryly with his eyes narrowed and hands on his hips. "Now who and what the hell was that?"

"Excuse me?" she asked, her eyes darting quickly back and forth.

"I saw you letting that man feel you up back there! Now who is him?"

"Huh? Oh, that's Domi..nic...and he was not feeling me up!"

Leticia swatted at De'Vyne playfully as she brushed past him and started towards the elevator. He kept pace with her, probing her with one question after another about the handsome stranger he spotted with her, and she ignored every one of them. All she would say is he was the new sound and lighting engineer replacing Emilio since he had vanished without a trace.

"Sound and lighting, huh? Well, I definitely saw a spark," De'Vyne said coyly with a sneaky smile, cutting his eyes at her.

"Oh, hush!" Leticia chastised jokingly as she watched the numbers of the elevator for what already felt like the hundredth time today. Leticia clutched the clipboard tightly to her chest as she quietly reflected on the feel of Dominic's warm hands on her body. Even though the moment was brief, it felt like time stood still and nothing else mattered except their closeness. There was a time when she used to dream of such a moment to be shared with Thee Domino Ballantyne, but now that she had, she wanted more. Leticia let out a dejected sigh as she stepped off the elevator because she knew that the desires and musings of her inner lovesick teenaged self were just that – fleeting and never gonna happen.

Chapter 3
'Twas ten days til...

• • ❧ • •

"Isn't that what you pay other people to do?" a distinct voice called out from below.

Leticia groaned and rolled her eyes before plastering a fake smile on her face as she looked down at her big sister, Edie, who was looking up with an unmistakable scowl of disgust.

"Hello to you too, Edie," Leticia said sarcastically. "And sometimes when you want it done right you have to do it yourself."

Leticia was on a ladder hanging strings of garland from the base of the balcony, draping them in loops as she went, when her sister arrived. They were supposed to be going to lunch, but she knew the real reason Edie came by was to spy on the progress being made with the Christmas party. Especially, since her husband's good name and reputation were attached to it.

Edie was apprehensive about the decision to use Leticia in the first place, but she was outvoted. Her husband, Hector, fully believed in his sister-in-law's skills for curating epic events, just based on her previous work. So, when he was tasked with putting something together for the mayor's office, Leticia was the first call he made, much to Edie's chagrin. Even though she told him it was a good idea, she wasn't really onboard, and her not-so-random pop-up visits were proof of that.

Leticia could see through Edie's false niceties of lunch invites and supply drop offs like glass, but opted not to let on that she knew her sister's true motives. She'd much rather successfully pull off this

16

Christmas party without a hitch and gloat about proving Edie wrong later than argue with her now.

"You're early," Leticia said, looking at her watch after she descended the ladder.

"Well, I was already in the area," Edie replied with a shrug.

"Already in the area? You live in Wicker Park," Leticia replied skeptically with a side-eye.

"What did I say?" Edie snapped, putting her hands on her hips.

Leticia rolled her eyes and said she couldn't leave right now because she was in the middle of a project. Edie huffed about them having this lunch date scheduled well-enough in advance that she shouldn't be getting excuses right now.

"It's not an excuse. You came too early," Leticia said flatly with a shrug as she climbed the ladder again.

"Oh, really, Late-ticia? Being too early is a problem, now?" Edie tossed back, rolling her neck and narrowing her eyes.

"You know I hate when you call me that!" Leticia exclaimed, nearly dropping the nail gun she was holding. "I was late one time! Let it go!"

"Nope."

As the two sisters continued their spat, the sound of Leticia's raised voice traveled across the room and caught Dominic's attention, making him pop up from inside the raised platform that would be the DJ's booth. He looked over to where the women were, and his eyes immediately became fixed on the curvature of Leticia's hips and butt in her dark blue jeans and the sliver of skin on her lower back that peeked out beneath the hem of her sweater each time she raised her arms to hang something.

Dominic licked and bit his bottom lip as he studied her every move. He didn't care at all if anyone else saw him watching her. Nothing could tear his eyes away from the woman who had swirled back into his life like a bodacious blizzard, taking his breath away at every turn. He looked forward to hearing her voice every day, even if it was just her rambling about her many checklists and deadlines. And her laugh? Music to his ears. However, right now there was a harshness in her tone that Dominic didn't like, because that meant someone was messing with "his Tecie Baby."

His brows knitted together as he frowned in anger, trying to figure out who the mystery woman was getting under Leticia's skin. Just then, Edie turned around and locked eyes with Dominic and he groaned loudly before crouching back down behind the DJ booth to finish working on the cords and switchboard.

"Is that..." Edie's voice trailed off as she squinted her eyes to make out the face she'd just seen across the room. "Leticia, tell me you did not hire that degenerate?"

"Who are you talking about?" Leticia grunted over her shoulder as she placed the last nail in the base to hang the rest of the garland.

"Domino Ballantyne," his name rolled off her tongue with such disdain.

"Oh...uh...yeah, he's the engineer," Leticia stated shyly.

"Engineer?! Him?! Not likely."

"Wow, Edie!"

The sound of approaching footsteps made them both turn around and Leticia instantly began smiling at how Dominic made something as simple as walking look so damn sexy. He had gotten a fresh haircut recently, so his handsome face was no longer covered by a baseball cap. Just the dewy glistening that sweat leaves behind after a long hard day of work — a look Leticia was becoming more and more grateful for.

"Hey, Tecie," Dominic interrupted the sisters' quarrel. "Here are your notes back from a few days ago. I keep forgetting to give them to you."

"Who the hell is Tecie?" Edie asked with a frown.

Dominic cut his eyes at her, never uttering a word as he passed her and stood at the base of the ladder. His scowl was steady as he slowly pulled his eyes away from Edie's face to look up at Leticia, who he quickly and sweetly smiled at as he handed over papers. She smiled back as she came down the ladder, stopping on the rung that brought her eye level to him.

Edie watched the silent exchange between the two of them and scoffed loudly, making Dominic's head snap back around to glare in her direction again. Leticia nervously dropped her eyes to the floor, wishing she could just liquify and disappear between the cracks.

"Always good to see you, Edith," Dominic snarled, using her real name.

"It's Edie, to you," she snarled in return.

"And it's Dominic, to you," he said sternly, looking her up and down and letting her know he'd heard her earlier comments about him.

Edie snorted and rolled her eyes as she waved him off and turned away from them. Leticia mouthed an apology to Dominic, who shook his head to say that wasn't necessary. He told her he needed to run out to his truck to get some more wiring for the DJ booth and grab a bite to eat. When Dominic asked if she wanted anything, Edie cut him off to say she was taking Leticia to lunch and that he needed to be more concerned with doing his actual job.

"Edie!" Leticia exclaimed, going red from embarrassment.

"Leticia don't be letting this...whatever you're supposed to be...get away with murder just 'cuz you're still carrying a torch for him," Edie said dismissively. "He is an employee. Treat him like one."

"Oh, my God! Domino, I am so sorry for this," Leticia apologized profusely, grabbing his arm. "You can go. Take all the time you need. It's okay."

Dominic looked up at the ceiling, took a long inhale and nodded his head as he exhaled a heavy breath — trying his hardest to keep his rage in check and not lash out at the woman hellbent on rubbing him the wrong way. He looked over at Leticia who was still clinging to his arm, and suddenly the comfort of that feeling settled the angry fire blazing inside him.

Dominic didn't want to leave her embrace, but knew he needed to get away from Edie as soon as possible. He nodded again and slipped out of Leticia's hands, brushing past Edie and glaring at her once more before leaving.

"What is wrong with you?!" Leticia asked angrily in Spanish as she slammed the stack of papers onto the utility cart beside her.

"Me?! What's wrong with you?!" Edie hurled back at her in Spanish. "Why would you let someone like that work with you? See, I knew it was a bad idea to have you do this party. Do you know who your client is?"

"Tell me how you really feel, Edie," Leticia said flippantly.

"Okay, I think you're in over your head with all of this and you're trying so hard to prove a point, that you're making piss poor business decisions, like working with the boy who terrorized our neighborhood for years."

"He terrorized you. He was always nice to me. And anyway, his past is none of my business. He's working now and he's actually very good at his job. Just like I'm damn good at my job. Not that you'd ever bother to notice."

Leticia grabbed a box of figurines and statuettes off the floor and marched to the other side of the room to begin placing the centerpieces on the tall tables situated around the perimeter. It was ten days until the big day and her catering team was coming tomorrow to finalize the menu and do a walkthrough to get a feel for the space and plan out how they'd navigate once it was filled with some of Illinois' political and social elite.

This week, alone, she had a full schedule of one vendor partner after another coming to the site to discuss all the particulars, which was stressful enough. The last thing she needed was Edie and any of her bullshit.

"You can go," Leticia said with her back still turned. "I've got a lot to do and don't have time for lunch right now."

"Lettie, you have to eat at some point. This stuff can wait," Edie said, rolling her eyes.

"Bye, Edie," Leticia snapped as she moved to the next table to set up the centerpieces.

Edie looked at the back of her sister's head in disbelief. She waited silently for Leticia to say something...anything...but she stayed quiet and kept on working. So, Edie loudly smacked her lips, gave a dry "Adios," and left without another word – much to Leticia's relief.

A light knock on her office door broke through Leticia's concentration while she was updating the PowerPoint with new photos of today's progress. Her heart skipped a beat when she saw Dominic standing there, bathed in the late afternoon sunlight streaming through the hall window behind him. He had changed out of his coveralls into a beige fitted, long-sleeved, thermal shirt; dark blue slim-fit jeans and wheat Timberland boots. His close-cropped dark hair glistened but they didn't hold a candle to the glint in his beautiful brown eyes that seemed to pierce her soul every time he looked at her.

"Hi," Leticia exhaled just above a whisper.

"Hi," Dominic's voice came from the depths of his throat.

"Wh-what are you still doing here? I thought you left already?" she asked with a slight tremble in her voice as she fidgeted with her pen.

"We didn't do our walkthrough for the day," he said, still hovering in the doorway.

"Oh, we don't have to today. I trust you."

"Hmm."

Dominic crossed the threshold to fully enter her office, walking slowly towards her desk. His long, lean arms hung at his sides and his abs flexed beneath his shirt with each step. The top two buttons were open, revealing a gold link chain and cross laid against the bronze skin of his toned chest. Leticia studied his every move, just like she did back in the day. His walk always mesmerized her, but it was no match for that thousand watt smile he would flash — just like he was doing now.

"At least one of you do," Dominic commented. "Hey, what's your sister's beef with me, anyway?"

"Please ignore her," Leticia replied, rolling her eyes and waving off any thoughts of Edie.

"Yeah, that's easier said than done," he said with a snort. "But, seriously, what's her deal? Did I do something to her that I don't remember?"

"I mean you did egg her one Halloween," she giggled.

"Well, shit!" he exclaimed with a chuckle.

Leticia explained that her sister's always had a bit of a judgmental attitude about other people, unfortunately, and especially anyone with any kind of troubled past.

"She doesn't believe people can change," Leticia explained, her chin resting on her fist. 'You are who you are,' she'd always say."

"And what do you think?" Dominic asked with a furrowed brow.

"I think people have the right to reinvent themselves as many times as they want until they find the version they like. That's what I do," she said, flashing a grin,

Dominic's eyes roamed over Leticia's face, absorbing every single detail. She had pulled her hair up into a messy bun with a few ringlets dangling around her face and purple wide-framed glasses took the place of her contacts. This was the "Tecie" he remembered. The quiet girl who sat in the back of the class, dazed, and doodling in her notebooks but somehow always knew the answer to every question, no matter the subject. That's who he saw each and every time he laid eyes on her — even now, and it always brought back heavy memories.

• • ⚓ • •

Summer '13 – Chicago
Leticia was blowing out the candles on her cake as her family and friends cheered. It was her college graduation/going-away party, and everyone had come together to celebrate. In a week, she would be leaving for New

York for a year-long paid internship at a premier interior design company, but Leticia secretly hoped this move would lead to something permanent. For now, she would enjoy spending the afternoon laughing, dancing and opening gifts surrounded by people who loved and would no doubt miss her terribly, but little did she know there was still someone missing...

Dominic had walked by Leticia's house at least eight times today, contemplating whether or not he should pop into the backyard and crash the party. Honestly, all he really wanted to do was see her. He knew this summer would be different than the last three since graduating high school. This might actually be their last one together, and the thought of that literally made him sick. So much so, that each time Dominic headed towards the backyard, he'd instantly get queasy.

"What the fuck is wrong with me?!" Dominic chastised himself as he paced back and forth on the walkway.

"Well, for starters you're out here talking to yourself," a transient voice called out behind him.

Dominic looked up on the porch and saw it was Leticia's older sister, Edie, scowling down at him. He grunted and shook his head in annoyance at the sight of her. The two of them had never gotten along and Dominic quit trying to figure out what her issue was ages ago. He waved his hand dismissively as he took a deep breath and made his way towards the back gate again.

"Uh, where are you going?!" Edie snapped as she angrily trotted down the porch steps.

"I'm going to the party," Dominic replied dryly, yanking his arm from her grasp when she reached for him.

"Oh no the hell you're not! You weren't invited!" she barked, pulling on the back of his shirt.

"I don't need an invite. It's me!"

"Which is exactly why you can't go back there!"

Edie jumped in front of Dominic, pushing firmly against his chest and halting his steps. He scoffed at the gesture and ordered her to get out of his way, but she adamantly refused.

"Domino, you don't want shit," Edie said firmly. "I've watched you toy with that girl's emotions and take advantage of her for years, and I'm sick of it. This party is for family and friends only. You're neither of those. So, go away!"

"She is my friend, Edie!" Dominic protested, still trying to get by.

"Yeah, but that doesn't mean you're hers. You knew Lettie had a crush on you and milked it for all it was worth. Never gave a damn about her, for real."

Just then, Leticia's face came into view through the crowd as she danced the Samba with one of her uncles. The way her face lit up as she laughed and twirled around almost made tears well up in Dominic's eyes. Edie's words cut him deeply and it was made worse by the possibility that Tecie thought the same things about him. Suddenly, he felt sick again.

"That's not true, Edie," Dominic pressed. "Tecie has always meant a lot to me, and since I may never see her again, I have to tell her how I feel now."

"Nope, it's too late for that," Edie said flatly, shaking her head. "Leticia is getting away from here and you. If you really felt something for my sister, you should've said it a long time ago. Now, go home, Domino."

Dominic looked down at Edie and then back at a smiling Leticia. She was so happy and had such a bright future ahead of her. Edie was right. He had waited too long. He was too late. For nearly eight years, Dominic had been so used to Leticia always being there, and now he was out of time. He stole one final glance at the sweetest face he'd ever laid eyes on, then dejectedly turned around to head home.

"You'll always be Tecie to me," Dominic said with a light shrug and a wink.

"And you'll always be Domino to me," she said, recalling the comment he'd made to Edie earlier and playfully sticking out her tongue.

"You can call me whatever you want," he replied in a sultry tone.

"You know, if I were a crazy woman, I'd swear you were flirting with me sometimes."

"You're not crazy...and you're not wrong."

Leticia sat erect as the shock of Dominic's words sent chills up her spine. Their eyes locked on each other, and a thick silence briefly filled the space between them. She was speechless, but incredibly curious to know exactly what he meant by that statement.

"Well, if there's nothing else you need from me, I guess I'll see you bright and early Monday morning," Dominic said with a soft huff and shrug as he started backing away.

"Uh...yeah, ok. S-see you Monday," Leticia stammered, still reeling.

Dominic stopped short when he reached the doorway and looked at Leticia over his right shoulder. She lifted her brows and tilted her head questioningly – a move that caused a knot to form in Dominic's chest as he gripped the doorjamb tightly.

"I carried a torch for you too, ya know," he said softly, remembering what Edie had revealed about Leticia earlier. "Still do."

With that, he disappeared into the hallway, leaving Leticia with her mouth dropped wide open and head spinning.

Chapter 4

'Twas six days til...

. . ⁓ . .

Dominic entered the event site, his heavy boots hitting the floor tiles with fervor and his eyes scanning the room like an Apex predator clocking its prey. He made note of every face he saw milling about, but once again the face he sought out the most was nowhere to be found. He exhaled a dejected sigh and made his way towards the electrical closet.

It had been almost a week since Dominic last saw Leticia face-to-face; since confessing his longtime secret crush, and now he had the distinct feeling she was avoiding him. Had he said too much? Did his words make her too uncomfortable to be around him now? Dominic was a man who prided himself on direct honesty, but maybe he had gone too far. Damn, I hope not, he mused to himself as he dropped his work bag to the floor.

The loud clang of the tools inside Dominic's bag made De'Vyne jump, then exhale a sigh of relief, because that was just the man he needed to see.

"Thank God you're here!" De'Vyne exclaimed, flailing his arms as he rushed over to Dominic.

"Good to see you too, D," Dominic replied jokingly as he knelt down and unzipped his tool bag.

"No, you don't understand," De'Vyne said, sounding out of breath. "We have a crisis, and I could really use your help."

"Me, specifically?"

26

"The one and only you."

Dominic looked up at De'Vyne with a skeptical expression and asked what the crisis was. It turns out there was an error made with the supply company they used to order a surplus of Christmas lights for the trees – they didn't send nearly enough lights.

"How many trees do you have and how tall are they?" Dominic asked, rising up from the floor.

"Four and they're all eighteen feet," De'Vyne said in a nervous tone.

"And how many feet of lights do you have?" Dominic inquired as they walked towards the center of the room.

"Eight hundred," De'Vyne replied with a painful grimace.

"Eight hundred?! That's it?!"

"That's it."

"Yeah, that ain't enough."

Dominic walked up to one of the bare trees, touching the branches to confirm it was artificial. He walked around it, peering between the branches trying to get a good look at the post. He did two laps around the tree before responding to De'Vyne's still unspoken plea for help.

"Y'all have a reimbursement clause in your contract with the city, right?" Dominic asked as he scanned the room once again to assess the other three trees.

"For any unexpected expenses incurred? Yeah," De'Vyne confirmed.

"Cool. You got a company card?" Dominic asked, cutting his eyes at him.

"Yeah," De'Vyne replied, raising his brow in suspicion.

"Good. You're gonna need it."

Dominic instructed De'Vyne to go to any nearby hardware store and get at least eight to ten more boxes of Christmas lights, or as many as he could find. He told him he had a plan in mind that should work, but they'd definitely need more strings of lights for it.

"Oh, and tell your team to stop decorating the trees until I get the lights up," Dominic instructed. "I don't wanna knock down or break shit I can't pay for."

"Okay. Thank you! Thank you, so much!" De'Vyne exclaimed as he squeezed him tight in a sideways hug.

"Don't thank me yet. This shit might not even work," Dominic said with a chuckle as he went to retrieve his ladder from the electrical closet.

"I'm praying it will," De'Vyne said as he walked away but stopped short to yell over his shoulder. "Oh, and pleeeaaassseee do not tell Leticia about this. She has enough on her plate right now. This might give her a stroke."

Dominic gave a silent thumbs up, as the mere mention of her name made a lump form his throat. When he first arrived at the jobsite, he wondered if she was even there today or working from home again, but now he knew for a fact she was in the building just like him. He quietly hoped for even just a glimpse of her face before he left for the day. They wouldn't even have to talk...he just needed to see her.

As he opened a box of the previously delivered lights and started untangling them, he smiled to himself and made a note to thank De'Vyne for pulling him into this so-called "crisis." Technically, Dominic's job of setting up the power banks and sound systems was nearly complete, and after today, he would have no further reason to be here. Which is why he hoped against hope that Leticia would show her gorgeous face today.

Dominic turned around to grab an extension cord from the utility cart beside him and jumped in surprise at the sight of a stern-faced Edie standing there.

"Where's my sister?" she asked pointedly with her arms folded across her chest.

"What is wrong with you?" Dominic asked in a disgusted tone as he shook his head.

"Excuse me?" she retorted, jerking her head back.

"You're rude as hell for like no reason," he started in an agitated tone. "No 'Good morning,' no 'How are you?' No nothing. Just come in barking orders and demands. What is wrong with you?!"

Dominic huffed and shook his head as he returned to his tasks of propping up the tall ladder and running the extension cord around the base of the tree. He could hear Edie scoffing and murmuring behind him, but resisted the urge to engage, until she decided to provoke him.

"You're demanding respect you don't deserve," Edie stated, her arms still folded.

"You are an em-ploy-ee. I bark orders, you comply. Period."

"First of all, Edie, fuck you," Dominic exhaled, his eyes narrowed. "I don't work for you, and even if I did, there would never be a day where you could talk to me outta the crack of your ass like you do."

"Excuse you?!" she exclaimed, clutching her pearls.

"No, excuse you. See, you think you know me, but you don't. You assume, and you know what they say about that."

Edie stepped forward to close the gap between them and drove a stiff finger into his sternum, as she berated him for speaking to her that. She told him she knew all there ever was to know about him and people like him. She said Leticia was a fool for entrusting some two-bit, ex-con to do any work for her and if she had any say-so about it, he wouldn't have been anywhere near this project.

"You are a menace to society, Domino," Edie said, poking him in the chest with each word. "And it doesn't matter how many years have passed or what uniform you put on. That's all you'll ever be."

"You're insane," Dominic said with a smirk. "Is that really what you think about me?"

"It's what I know," she replied in a defiant tone.

"Then you don't know shit. Edie, I've never been to prison a day in my life. Never been to juvie, either. Hell, I've never even been to court for anything other than a traffic ticket."

Dominic told her not only did he not have a prison record, but he had actually gone to college straight out of high school just like everybody else. However, he couldn't afford to finish, so he only did two years. From there, he went to work for his uncle at his auto shop where he learned how to install custom sound systems in cars. Dominic enjoyed the work so much, he decided that's what he wanted to do as a career. His uncle supported his dream and paid for him to go back to school to finish his engineering degree and get his state certification.

"I'm an educated Black man with an honest trade and my own business with a healthy clientele," Dominic continued. "I have a bomb ass résumé, not a prison record. So, like I said, you don't know shit about me."

Edie blinked rapidly as she processed Dominic's words. Before she could respond, she heard Leticia's voice behind her and slowly turned away from Dominic to lock eyes with her sister.

"Edie, what are you doing here?" Leticia asked as she walked over to them, purposely avoiding Dominic's gaze.

"Uh...I came to see you," Edie stammered, still trying to recover from her exchange with Dominic. "You haven't been answering my calls or responding to texts. So, I came to check on you."

"I'm fine, Edie," Leticia said dryly, still feeling a little perturbed from their row a few days ago.

Hell yeah, you are, Dominic thought to himself as he watched her out of the corner of his eye. The sight of her smooth, plump calves and the peek-a-boo of fleshy thighs under the hem of her dress made his mouth water. Today was the first time she hadn't worn pants to work, and he could not be more grateful.

Leticia's horchata complexion covered in the dark maroon material was the perfect contrast. The dress stopped at mid-thigh with large pleats and flowed outward, which only accentuated her curvy hips and butt more. The top of the dress hugged her ample bosom, making her breasts sit up higher than she probably intended, but everything about it was perfect in Dominic's eyes.

Begrudgingly, he tore his eyes away from her and started ascending the ladder with the ream of lights draped around his arm — an act that instantly caught her attention.

"Uh, what are you doing?" Leticia asked, holding up a finger to halt Edie's next words.

"Climbing a tree," Dominic said sarcastically over his shoulder.

"And why are you climbing a tree?" she pressed further in her own sarcastic tone.

"Because I was asked to, Tecie."

"By who?"

Just then De'Vyne came rushing back into the room with multiple Home Depot bags dangling from his arms and sweat pooling on his forehead. When he spotted Leticia standing there, he murmured a flood of curse words under his breath as he walked towards her.

"H-Hey, Boss Lady," De'Vyne stuttered as he sat the bags down on the floor.

"De'Vyne, what are you up to and why?" Leticia interrogated with her hands on her hips and eyes fixed on her assistant.

De'Vyne exhaled a heavy sigh and told her about the fiasco with the Christmas lights. The more he talked, the wider her eyes got and the louder her, "What?!" became. As she started to fuss and curse in Spanish with her arms flailing in the air, De'Vyne tried to reassure her that there was a perfectly good solution in the works.

"What possible solution could there be that won't make this a shitshow in six days?!" Leticia exclaimed angrily.

"This," De'Vyne said cheerfully as he pulled a box of lights from one of the bags.

"How does that help me, De'Vyne?!" she demanded.

"It doesn't," Dominic interrupted as he reached past her to take the box and look it over. "It helps me."

Dominic explained that he and De'Vyne had a plan, and that Leticia could rest assured nothing else would or could go wrong — at least not with the Christmas trees.

"Dominic, this isn't your problem," Leticia said with an exasperated breath.

"It's a lighting problem. I'm the lighting guy. Thus, it's my problem," Dominic said matter-of-factly.

"But you didn't come here to be bothered with Christmas trees," she groaned.

"I came here to help you. Let me help you, Tecie," he replied softly with the twinkle of a smile in his eyes.

"I...okay," she relented.

Leticia, Edie and De'Vyne walked away to let Dominic get on with his plan to remedy the lights situation, and as she went, he watched the sway of her hips with every step. Leticia could feel the heat of his gaze caressing her waistline and it made her spine go rigid as she stole a glance at him on the way out of the room. Their eyes met briefly, and he didn't even bother to avert or pretend as if he wasn't watching her. He just threw her a wink which made her face immediately flush red before she disappeared out of sight.

Several hours later, Dominic was packing up his work bag when he heard steps approaching behind him. He looked over his shoulder and saw De'Vyne breezing towards him with a smile on his face.

"Aye, man, you all out of favors for the day," Dominic tossed over his shoulder as he hoisted his bag up off the ground

"Ha! That's not even why I'm here," De'Vyne laughed as he brought his hand from behind his back and passed him a pristine white envelope.

"What's that?" Dominic asked with a furrowed brow.

"It's an official invite to the Christmas party next Friday," De'Vyne said gleefully.

He told Dominic how grateful he was for all his help with the Christmas lights earlier and how much of a relief it was to Leticia, as well. The whole team appreciated all of his hard work and always having the perfect solution to any problem right in his back pocket over the past two weeks.

"I know you came here just to work on sound and lights, but you did so much more for us, and we just wanted to thank you for it," De'Vyne explained as he happily clasped his hands together in front of him.

"Damn, thank you, man," Dominic said graciously with a wide smile. "Y'all didn't have to do this, but I really appreciate it."

"You deserve it."

"Thanks."

The two of them shook hands and Dominic headed out. When the doors opened to one of the elevator cars, he saw Leticia standing there bathed in the warm fluorescent lighting inside. She stared at him with a longing she was too afraid to express and parted her lips to say words she ached to say, but nothing came out. So, she smiled awkwardly and stepped off the elevator, brushing past him. The scent of her sweet perfume invaded his senses, making him moan low in his throat.

"Oh, wait," Leticia called out to him. "Tonight's your last night, right?"

"Yeah, you're officially rid of me," Dominic replied with a slight smirk.

"Don't say it like that," she said with a giggle. "But thank you so much for everything. Literally could not have done this without you."

"That's nice of you to say. Glad I could be of service," he said in a low voice.

The depth of his raspy baritone snaked its way through her ears and worked its way through her torso, settling in her core and making her cross her legs at the ankles and pinch her thighs together. Trying to maintain her self-control, Leticia switched gears and asked if he had received his invitation. When he said he had, she told him how much she looked forward to seeing him in his masquerade costume next week.

"You could see me sooner, if you're interested," Dominic said in a hopeful tone.

"What do you mean?" Leticia asked with a shaky voice, her legs still locked together.

"Go on a date with me, Tecie," he said pointedly.

"A what?" her voice barely above a whisper.

"A date. You know, dinner? A movie? Ice skating at Maggie Daley Park? A date."

For what felt like an eternity, Leticia stood there in stunned silence, exhaling one trembling breath after another. Dominic held her gaze captive as he waited with his own bated breath for her answer. He took a step forward to be closer to her, to emphasize the seriousness of his request and his need to hear her say "Yes." Leticia's eyes fluttered closed as Dominic's body heat washed over her from his closeness.

She inhaled a deep breath when she felt Dominic brush a wisp of hair from her forehead. The spice and musk of his cologne penetrated her nose and made her whole body tingle. Pressing her thighs together was no longer working and her knees immediately felt weak when Dominic whispered her name to get her to look at him.

Her eyelids flew open, and she was immediately met with the pleading that lay in Dominic's brown eyes. So badly, she wanted to cup his face in her hands. To pull his perfect blush pink lips to hers and finally know what they taste like. To feel his strong hands clutching her waist again like they did on that first day. So badly, she wanted so much...but she couldn't.

"I can't," Leticia said simply, almost sounding remorseful.

"You can't? Dominic asked, trying to understand.

"I can't," she repeated softly, her eyes begging him not to make her explain further.

"Because we work together, right? I get it," he replied quietly with a nod.

Dominic leaned forward and pressed his lips to her left cheek, letting them linger for a moment. As he pulled away, he whispered, "Goodbye, Leticia," and walked backwards to the elevator. The sound of her name on his lips attached to a "Goodbye" caused a painful sting in her heart. It had been over a decade since they'd last seen each other and who knows if or when they'll ever see each other again.

As the doors closed, Leticia's bottom lip began to quiver as she blinked back tears. She shook her head, trying to dispel the emotions bubbling up inside her. Not being able to stand the sight of the numbers above the elevator tick backwards any longer, Leticia quickly spun on her heels and headed towards the event space to do her nightly walkthrough before going home.

The moment Leticia stepped into the room, her hands flew to her mouth. The four green trees were fully decorated with various ornaments, candy canes; gold, silver, red and green foil tinsel draped across the branches. The glass ornaments and baubles flickered and danced in the light, instantly drawing your attention to them. There were miniature masquerade masks adorning two of the trees, giving them a bit of a Mardi Gras aesthetic, just like the theme of the party. Atop each tree was a Swarovski crystal star that flashed iridescently, but what really made Leticia's heart swell was the lighting.

Dominic had wrapped the posts of the trees in strands of multicolored lights. There was a remote attached with a control dial he had set to "Dancing," which made the lights blink to their own rhythm. They illuminated the trees from the inside out and from the very top all the way to the base. The issue of not having enough lights earlier was now nonexistent.

Leticia's eyes welled up with tears once again as she squealed in excitement. At that moment, she truly saw the fruits of her labor coming together, and started to believe that this party would go exactly as planned. She rushed into De'Vyne's arms, and they squeezed each other tight as they celebrated closing in on the finish line of this project.

"This looks amazing!" Leticia squealed as she went up to one of the trees, gingerly touching the ornaments.

"That man is a miracle worker! Because I did not expect this," De'Vyne exclaimed as he peered between the branches at the dancing lights.

"That he is," she agreed in a hushed tone.

"So, you still playing hard-to-get or nah?" he asked, cutting his eyes at her and smirking.

"Am I what?!"

"Oh, Miss Ma'am, even a blind man can see the fireworks between y'all two. Now, I know you got that weird rule about not dating people you work with, buuuuttt now he's not working with you. Soooo...?"

Leticia slowly pulled her hand away from the tree and dropped her eyes to the floor at De'Vyne's question. The slump in her shoulders made him concerned and he asked if everything was okay, but when she revealed Dominic had asked her out and she said "No," he let her have it.

"You what?!" De'Vyne exclaimed. "Why?!"

"Because in what world do I actually get a guy like that?" Leticia asked, her voice cracking.

"In this one!" he said plainly. "That man wants you. Even I know that. And now, so do you. Call him, tell him you're full of shit and you're sorry. Then say yes."

"I can't, Dev. I just can't," she said, shaking her head.

"You can. You're just scared. My question is why, though?"

As they walked back to her office, Leticia told De'Vyne of her history with Dominic. Their years at Jefferson High School, always having at least one class together every semester for four years straight. Living on the same block for years and seeing him shirtless all summer as he roamed their street every day. She had the biggest crush on him and tried so hard not to be obvious about it, but knew she failed miserably every day.

Leticia would blush and giggle like a maniac every time Dominic even spoke to her, and Edie would get so mad at her for it. "He's just a boy! Get yourself together!" she'd yell constantly.

The embarrassment Leticia felt when her sister said that was nothing compared to the pain she'd feel seeing Dominic with other girls around the neighborhood; but it was always soothed by the fact that no matter who he was with or what he was doing, he made it a point to speak to her. Whether in class or sitting on her front porch, Dominic Ballantyne was guaranteed to say, "Tecie, boo! What it do?!" each and every time.

She told De'Vyne that even though Dominic was what some may consider popular in high school with a bit of a bad boy edge, he was always sweet to her. He defended her when other people teased her. Whenever he saw her sitting alone, he'd come over and join her. Dominic would come to her first when he needed help with homework, and she always laughed at how excited he got seeing her after her Food & Nutrition class because he knew she was coming with snacks. He even told her one day, "I hope you know, you've spoiled me, and you're stuck with me," when she had made him peanut butter cookies.

"Sounds to me like he was putting his bid in even back then," De'Vyne said with a side-eye.

"No, he was just being nice to the nerdy, fluffy girl," Leticia said with a dejected shrug.

"Boss Lady, I mean this with all my love and respect," he started. "But you're still nerdy and fabulously fluffy."

"Well, gee, thanks," she replied gruffly, rolling her eyes.

"No, hear me out. You are gorgeous with cheekbones I'd kill for. The girls be sittin' and the booty be poppin', honey! You got body-on-body that's soft, supple and plush in all the best places. Big legs, full lips and luxurious hair. You always give 'naughty librarian' mixed with 'shy virgin energy,' that would drive any man crazy. And that man wants you, in every way! Trust me."

De'Vyne encouraged Leticia once again to give Dominic a call and a chance, because he deserves and so does she. Leticia pondered on his words, still feeling unsure. Does Dominic really like me like that? Or is he just a man who likes to flirt? But why would he ask you out if he wasn't for real? Eh, maybe he was just being nice like always. Her thoughts funneled through her mind like water swirling down the drain.

• • ⚜ • •

The confusion and uncertainty of a man's true feelings and intentions were one of the main reasons why Leticia hated the dating scene and just hurled herself into her work. Now, the lines between those two worlds were blurred with the arrival of Dominic Ballantyne, and she was more confused than ever.

Then as Leticia reached the doorway of her office and flicked off the light, suddenly Dominic's voice echoed in her head. "I carried a torch for you too. Still do." Leticia's eyes widened as that realization set in. Domino wants me?! she thought to herself. Carried a torch for me?! Asked me on a date and I said "No?!"

"The fuck is wrong with me?!" she chastised herself as she pulled her cellphone out of her purse and scrolled until she found Dominic's number.

Chapter 5

'Twas the night of...

. . ❧ . .

De'Vyne handed Leticia the mirror to assess her makeup as he adjusted the straps of her dress and secured the zipper. She donned a royal blue satin, off-the-shoulder gown with corset bodice and mermaid skirt. Her hair was pulled up in a fauxhawk with rhinestones pinned throughout.

Leticia smiled with joy at De'Vyne's handiwork. Her eyeshadow was a smokey blend of silver, black and blue with full lashes and glittery eyeliner on her lower lid. Pink-tinted nude lipstick with brown lipliner created an ombre hue on her lips, and blush was lightly brushed across her cheekbones.

"This looks amazing! Thank you!" she gushed while leaning on his shoulder as he helped with her shoes.

"I had to make sure my girl looked phenomenal on her big night!" De'Vyne replied with a wink.

"And so do you," she complimented.

"Well, you know," he said with the click of his tongue as he dragged the pad of his middle finger across his perfectly arched eyebrow.

De'Vyne wore a metallic silver shirt with a large bow collar and bell sleeves, black slim-fit slacks and silver Christian Louboutin loafers. His makeup was just as bold with feathery lash extensions and glitter adorning his cheekbones. The two of them looked exquisite for tonight's festivities.

40

The Mayor's Christmas Masquerade Party to benefit the City Colleges of Chicago and Chicago Public Schools had finally arrived and Leticia could not be more excited. Over the last two weeks, she was sure she'd lose her mind trying to pull this off, but tonight her very own Christmas miracle was coming to fruition.

Leticia picked up her blue mask with gold and silver glitter and feathered adornments from her desk, hooked her arm in De'Vyne's and they headed upstairs to the enclosed rooftop. Music vibrated through the hallway as they stepped off the elevator and rounded the corner to see attendees mingling just outside the room.

The room was full of partygoers, some in masks and some just in dramatic makeup, dressed to the nines and imbibing on the open bar and floating trays of champagne. There were aerial dancers suspended from the rafters, spinning and twirling to the musical stylings of the DJ across the room. The Christmas trees illuminated the four corners of the room beautifully, and no one would ever know the secret of making that happen.

Leticia spotted Edie and Hector and separated from De'Vyne to go greet them.

"There she is!" her brother-in-law, Hector, cheered in Spanish when he spotted her.

"Hey, Bro!" Leticia said excitedly back in Spanish as they hugged tightly.

"This looks amazing! I knew you could pull it off," he praised.

"Whew! It definitely was an experience," she exhaled heavily with a laugh.

"Congrats, Lettie. You did a wonderful job," Edie chimed in from beside her husband.

Leticia eyed her sister suspiciously at first, unsure if her praises were genuine or not, but the proud smile on her face was confirmation enough. The sisters embraced each other, rocking side-to-side gleefully. Hector took Leticia around to introduce and brag about her to some of the premier guests in attendance, namely the mayor and a slew of Commissioners and Directors for the city.

Her head was spinning, face hurting from smiling and eyes struggling to readjust after a barrage of cameras flashing in her face for the last hour. Leticia was finally able to break away from the crowd and get to the bar, where she spotted De'Vyne stirring his martini.

"The woman of the hour! You look like you need a drink," he chuckled.

"You have no idea!" she laughed back as she ordered a cranberry and vodka cocktail.

When her drink arrived, the two of them clinked their glasses to another successful Leticia Nadal Production. They watched the crowd dance and revel in the festive entertainment provided for the night. Just as De'Vyne spotted Edie and Hector dancing together, a thought occurred to him.

"So, where's mister man this evening?" he asked, referring to Dominic.

"Probably not coming since I blew it with him," Leticia said dejectedly as she polished off her drink and ordered a refill.

"What do you mean?" he asked, raising a dramatic eyebrow.

"Because I never called after turning down his date invite," she revealed and quickly kept talking, preventing De'Vyne from laying into her. "I chickened out that night, and every day after that, I just kept making excuses not to call him. Now here we are a week later, and I still haven't called."

"Guess that explains the no RSVP."

"Yup."

Like De'Vyne, Leticia had been watching the event queue to see if Dominic would officially accept their party invite and RSVP, even though she rejected his date request. Secretly, she hoped he would at least show up so she could apologize for being such a chicken before and ask him out instead. She found herself watching the door every time someone new walked in, and instantly felt the pain of disappointment at it not being him.

"Yeah, so, Merry, Merry or whatever," Leticia sighed sarcastically as she downed her second drink.

"I still think you should call him, or at least text," De'Vyne suggested, giving her a side-eye.

"Nah, it's too late for that," she replied, sounding sad.

"It's never too late to go for what you want, Ma'am, and that includes a fine ass man," he punctuated his statement with a playful hip bump before sashaying away into the crowd to dance with someone that had piqued his own interest.

Leticia laughed lightly at his last words but pondered on the weight of them. Could De'Vyne be right about there still being a chance with Dominic? Or was the sting of her rejection too much to recover from? There was only one way to find out. She pushed off from the bar, whizzing through the throng of attendees to head out the door, but bumped into her sister.

"Where's the fire?" Edie asked playfully in Spanish.

"Girl, you know how surgically attached I am to my cell phone," Leticia replied jokingly. "I feel so naked right now. I'm just running down to my office. I'll be right back."

"Okay, but don't be gone too long. Hector has a surprise for you," Edie hinted with a wink.

"Ooohh! Well, let me hurry up!" Leticia squealed as she dashed into the hallway.

Leticia made it to the elevators just as the doors opened and a crowd exited heading to the party. She spoke to a few people she recognized and waited for everyone to get off before she got on. Just as the crowd dissipated, one lone passenger remained, standing at the back, leaning against the wall with his hands in his pockets. It was something in the way he looked at her, even through his black and silver half-mask, that set Leticia's skin on fire. She knew exactly who it was.

She stared in awe at Dominic Ballantyne, who stood there just as cool and calm as ever, draped in a midnight blue suit that shimmered in the elevator lighting. The dark color against his golden skin was immaculate. His neatly trimmed beard framed perfect lips that curled into a subtle smirk as his eyes swept over Leticia's body, from top to bottom and back again.

"Aren't you going to the party?" Leticia asked nervously, trying to steady her breathing and pointing towards the hall.

"I go where you go," Dominic said, his voice low, husky and caressing every inch of her ear.

Leticia softly gasped at the directness of his statement and tried, but to no avail, hiding her smile as she stepped on the elevator. She could feel the heat of his eyes on the bare skin of her back that was visible through her dress. It was so intense, it might as well have just been his actual hands – not that she would mind if it was. They took the elevator ride in silence, enveloped in thick tension and pheromones.

They departed at the thirty-fourth floor, with Dominic leisurely following behind Leticia, watching the sway of her hips. His hands were still in his pockets and his loafers clicked along the tiles, matching each step she took. The echoes were the only sounds made until they reached her office.

"I didn't think I'd see you tonight," Leticia finally said, breaking through the silence as she walked over to her desk.

"Why? You invited me, remember?" Dominic inquired as he closed the door and leaned against it.

"Yeah, but you never RSVP'd. So, I thought you weren't coming," she said over her shoulder.

"Ah...Well, you know how much I hate following rules," he answered, smiling coyly.

Leticia giggled at the memory of their high school days and all the times she witnessed him getting in trouble for defying one rule or another without any remorse or regret.

"Yeah, you did have a little problem with authority," Leticia teased. "I don't know how you survived working for me these last few weeks."

"I'd gladly let you boss me around anytime you want," Dominic said plainly, his eyes piercing her soul.

Leticia inhaled sharply once again, her lungs stinging and reminding her to breathe. She dropped her eyes to the desk, spotting her cell phone, which was the only reason she was down there anyway. It would be so easy to just grab it and go back to the party, but she'd wanted this moment alone with Dominic for nearly a week.

"Domino, I owe you an explanation," she began.

"For?" Dominic asked, a slight frown marring his features as he pulled off his mask.

"For turning you down last week," she said softly.

"Nah, you don't have to explain your 'No' to me. I respect it," he replied with a light shrug, driving his hands back in his pockets and adjusting his posture against the door.

"You probably won't after I tell you why I said it," she said quietly.

Leticia walked around her desk, coming to stand in the middle of the floor. She removed her own mask, so he could fully see the sincerity in her eyes as she explained her hesitancy to respond to his advances. She confessed her uncertainty, and maybe even a bit of insecurity where Dominic was concerned.

"I never know if you're flirting because you're just being nice or toying with me," Leticia admitted as she fidgeted with the strings of her mask in her hands.

"Why would I be toying with you?" Dominic asked, narrowing his eyes.

"I don't know why you would, but I guess it's the same as when we were kids," she said. "You used to act all cute and flirty with me back then too, but I knew you weren't serious. I just thought you were being nice...or maybe just playing a joke."

Dominic turned his head to look away from her, trying to process what she'd just said. No matter how many times he'd imagined this scenario and conversation, he never saw it going this way. Her words pierced his eardrums and his heart, because Leticia really thought there was no way he'd genuinely flirt with or be interested in her. The realization of that was more painful than Dominic could've ever imagined.

His silence was deafening to Leticia and suddenly she felt awkward and way too exposed by her confession that he'd yet to respond to. Especially with him not even bothering to look her in the eyes right now. She couldn't take it anymore and immediately regretted the entire exchange. Leticia dropped her arms in embarrassed defeat and walked to the door, attempting to push past Dominic and reach for the doorknob. What happened next was the last thing she ever expected.

Dominic snaked his arm under Leticia's and slowly moved it up her body until his palm came to rest against her throat. Gently squeezing the pulse on each side of her neck as he caressed the side of her face with his breath. When Leticia felt his soft lips on the skin of her neck just along her hairline, she let out a soft whimper. Her forehead and palms were pressed to the door and knees locked together the second she felt that familiar pulsing between her legs.

With Dominic's hard body pinned to her back and pelvis pushing into her soft ass, Leticia was literally between a rock and a hard place, and right now she couldn't tell which was which. The wetness of Dominic's tongue trailing along the space between her neck and collarbone was such a sensual shock to her system that she moaned his name loudly before she could stop herself.

"Dominic..." his real name slid across her lips like a cool ice cube.

"Mmmm...Yes, Le-ti-ci-a?" Dominic growled hers just as ravenously as he felt, elongating every syllable.

He inhaled the scent of her hair – hibiscus and strawberries – and became hypnotized by the woman wedged between him and the office door. He sank so easily into her soft body, that he could only imagine what it would feel like to become completely lost in her.

Leticia moaned again as she felt Dominic's erection grow harder, pressing firmly into her ass. Involuntarily, her hips began grinding against him, making Dominic tighten his grip around her throat as he released a visceral groan of his own into her ear. She knew if they didn't stop now, they'd reach the point of no return, and she couldn't allow that to happen. Not here. Not with him.

Leticia pushed off the door and turned around to face Dominic. Now that they were face-to-face, she nearly lost her nerve. Especially, once he placed his palms at either side of her head on the door. His face hovered over hers and he absorbed everything she was in that moment. The dark brown of her eyes and how they contrast to her smooth vanilla skin. The rounded fullness of her face that he always wanted to trace with his finger, right down to the rise and fall of her plump breasts as she took one quickened, nervous breath after another.

Dominic leaned forward, touching the tip of his nose to hers, but before his lips could follow suit, he felt her small hand collide into his chest. He looked down at it, then back to her eyes, tilting his head in confusion. Leticia slipped under his right arm and walked away from him on wobbly legs. She stopped short in front of her desk and spun on her heels when she heard footsteps coming up behind her.

"Stop." Leticia said firmly with her arm outstretched.

"Did I do something wrong?" Dominic asked, stopping so abruptly that his shoes squeaked across the floor tile.

"This," she said, shaking her head. "This can't happen."

"Why not?" he asked, trying to hide a smirk. "Because we're at work?"

"Because it's not real!"

Dominic's posture went rigid, eyes narrowed, and lips pursed at Leticia's words. He shoved his hands back into his pockets and watched her in stoic silence for a moment – partly pondering on what she had said and partly to see if she'd say more. Now it was her muteness that screamed at infinite volumes.

"Why is it so hard for you to believe how I feel about you?" Dominic asked after a while, his voice firm and direct.

"Maybe because I don't know how you actually feel about me," Leticia retorted in a snappy tone.

"I feel like you're the most beautiful woman I've ever known, and I don't just mean physically," he started. "You are sweet and way too caring about people who don't deserve an ounce of your kindness. I've honestly always thought that, even back in high school."

Leticia watched closely as Dominic took a step forward, being sure to keep his movements slow and calculated.

"I feel like your smile has always been my favorite feature," Dominic continued. "Next one is your eyes, because of how you see me when no one else ever has."

Leticia sat on the edge of her desk and listened intently to his every word, clinging to the desire to believe each one of them. Her heart started racing again, like it did when their bodies were fused together at her office door. This time he had her pinned in place by his vulnerability and blunt honesty – a welcomed pressure she'd gladly fall under.

"I feel that this newfound confidence you have is so fucking sexy," Dominic admitted. "Honestly, it's just an extension of the sexiness I've always felt you had. It makes it damn near impossible to be around you every day because it's so hard not to touch you. Probably the hardest thing I've ever had to deal with in my life."

Dominic walked forward some more, closing the gap between them and finally being back within arm's reach.

"I want you, Leticia Nadal," he stated plainly. "That's how I feel about you. Now you know."

He watched closely as Leticia's body relaxed and she exhaled a heavy sigh. Her eyes fluttered quickly as the gravity of his words settled in her mind. Leticia repeatedly parted her lips to speak, but nothing would come out. Dominic's eyes were fixed on her like a cheetah eyeing its prey – intense, focused, and unwavering.

Searching her eyes for an answer to the question that lay in his own, Dominic slowly licked his lips and felt a jolt in his loins when he saw her do the same.

He leaned in close, brushing his coarse beard against her cheek as he inhaled the heady scent along her neck and moaning softly near her ear when he felt her hands slip inside his suit jacket and grip his ribs. "I want to kiss you so bad, but I don't wanna mess up your lipstick," Dominic whispered, looking deep into her eyes.

"It's smudge proof," Leticia whispered back with a smile tugging at her lips.

"Oh, thank God." he softly exclaimed as he cupped her face in his hands and captured her mouth with his own.

The fleshiness of their lips joined together, as his tongue massaged hers and their breathing grew heavier. Dominic kissed Leticia with all the longing he'd ached with for over a decade. He always wondered what it would be like to kiss her, and now that he was, nothing could make him stop. Leticia's small hands caressed his torso so tenderly as she finally allowed herself to succumb to the wilds of Dominic Ballantyne, but for her, kissing wasn't enough.

Leticia traced Dominic's lips with her tongue, then captured his bottom lip between her teeth. He groaned with pleasure as he slid his hand from her face and gripped her throat again, a move that made her smile sinisterly. He turned her head slightly to give himself full access to the left side of her neck, and he began drawing circles along her pulse with the tip of his tongue. Her grip on him tightened and the throbbing in her core intensified. Panting in ecstasy and her eyes full of fire and passion, Leticia needed more.

"Make love to me," she demanded in a breathy whisper against his ear.

"Mmm, I'd love to, baby," Dominic moaned against her neck. "But you have a party to get back to."

"So?" she retorted in a high-pitched voice, her eyes darting around in confusion.

"So, me making love to you requires I leave no part of your body untouched," he explained slowly. "That I discover all the different ways to make you cum over...and over...and over. And you don't have that kinda time. Not right now, anyway."

Dominic smirked and brushed his knuckles along her cheek and jawline as he spoke – a combination that only made her want him more. His voice made her blood run hot like lava coursing through her veins, and she could no longer press her knees and thighs together to ward off the horniness she felt.

"Maybe not," Leticia began. "But you do have time to fuck me."

"What?" Dominic asked abruptly, his smile fading and hand freezing in midair.

"Fuck...Me...Domino," she commanded as she leaned in closer with each word until her breast were pressed against his abs.

Dominic's smile returned and his eyes darkened as he gripped the back of her head and covered her mouth with his once again, this time with much more hunger and ferocity. He told her she could boss him around anytime, and he meant it. It was at this very moment he realized just how much of a turn on it was.

"Yes, ma'am," he said seductively against her lips.

He undid the single button on his jacket and Leticia pushed the material off his shoulders and down his arms, tossing it on the chair next to them. Dominic pulled Leticia to her feet and turned her around. He kissed the top of her spine and shoulder blades as he eased down the zipper of her dress and pushed the straps down her arms until it became a pool of satin at her feet. He picked it up and tossed it into the chair with his jacket.

Leticia stood there in a black lace one-piece body shaper that accentuated her curves. Dominic's hands caressed the skin of her hips, ass, and thighs as he nipped at the sensitive area at the back of her neck. Leticia bit her bottom lip as the feel of his hands on her body aroused her to the highest level. She turned around to face him and started unbuttoning his shirt while he bent down to kiss and caress her cleavage.

Dominic hooked his fingers through the straps of the body shaper and started pulling them down, until Leticia stopped him.

"It actually has snaps," she said, pointing down between her legs.

"Merry Christmas to me," Dominic replied with a devilish grin, his voice deep and sultry.

He pulled out the other empty chair beside them, turned Leticia towards it and instructed her to put her knees in the seat, which she did happily. As she did, Dominic spotted a spool of red tinsel on her desk and got an idea. He encircled his arm around her waist and pressed his lips close to her ear.

"You still trust me, right?" he asked, stroking her arm with the knuckles of his free hand.

"Yes, I trust you," Leticia said with a shaky breath.

Dominic tilted her head back and kissed her deeply as he slid his hand from around her waist to between her legs. Finding the snaps of her one-piece, he popped them open in one smooth motion and slipped his middle finger through the opening, sliding it along the slit of her lips until they parted. The second she felt his finger rub against her clit, Leticia's back arched and she let out a throaty moan. Dominic drew circles along her clit with the pad of his finger while cupping her breasts with his other hand, holding her close as he touched and teased her.

Leticia's body jerked and she grabbed his arm tightly, signaling that she just orgasmed because of him for the very first time. The knowledge of that made Dominic insanely hard and he could no longer resist being inside of her. He released his hold on her and grabbed the tinsel he had spotted. Coming around the chair to stand in front of her, he unraveled the tinsel and smiled as her eyes widened with the realization of what he had planned.

Dominic kissed her once more, wrapped the tinsel one time around each of her wrists and then tied the ends around the back legs of the chair; leaving Leticia leaned over the back of the chair with her ass in the air and spine perfectly arched. She giggled the entire time at how excited he was to tie her up with Christmas tree tinsel, of all things.

When he finished tying her up, he went to stand behind her. After a short while of nothing happening, Leticia asked if everything was alright, and he told her he was just enjoying the view. She giggled, making her plump butt jiggle slightly and it drove him wild. Dominic slapped her cheeks with both hands, biting his lip and moaning each time he did. Then he pulled down his pants and boxers, pushed back the open flaps of his shirt and moved closer to Leticia until his hard erection teased at the opening of her wet pussy.

"What do you want me to do again?" Dominic asked slyly as he continued rubbing his dick against her lips and clit.

"Mmm...fuck me, Domino," she moaned as she wiggled her hips and butt again.

"Gladly," he moaned in return as he slid inside of her with ease – like he belonged there.

The second he felt the wetness and warmth of her flesh wrapped around him, Dominic took in a long sip of air and gripped her hips fiercely. He wasn't ready for it to feel like this. He'd admit there had been fantasies and imaginings, but now that he was in it, he was fighting like hell to stay in it. The recoil of her hips and ass from every thrust he gave, the way her walls clenched around him, the sound of their skin slapping together echoing throughout the office – all of it sent Dominic's heart racing and blood boiling.

Leticia pressed her face into the cushion of the chairback to muffle her screams of pleasure as Dominic moved in and out of her core, pushing her further over the edge each time he entered. The curve of his dick hit her G-Spot dead center on every thrust, and Leticia lost count of how many times she had cum. Her toes curled tightly inside her shoes as Dominic worked her body.

Between the feel of his thick dick in her pussy and her being restricted by the makeshift bondage, her orgasms were more intense than she'd ever known before. She released a scream from deep within her chest as another surge rushed through her body.

Dominic dug his nails into her lush flesh as he felt the knot forming low in his abdomen, signaling he was close to losing it. Sweat poured down his chest and pooled around his pelvis as it slapped against her skin over and over. The heat of their passion was everything he thought it would be and then some.

"Fuck, Tecie!" Dominic groaned loudly as he thrust harder. "I knew you had some good ass pussy!"

"Oh...my...fucking...God!" Leticia cried with each thrust as she gripped the legs of the chair tightly and gave over to another shattering orgasm.

The sensation of her walls clenching his manhood again was the last straw. Dominic sped up his movements, pushing harder and faster until he found his own release – exhaling a barrage of curse words each time his body spasmed in ecstasy. He collapsed forward, his head falling right in the center of Leticia's back. They both fell into a euphoric giggle fit as they rode out the last of their sexual high.

"Perfect! No one will ever know I ravaged you," Dominic said playfully as he adjusted the straps of her dress.

"Yeah, but they may know about me ravaging you," Leticia joked as she tried smoothing out the wrinkles in his shirt.

"Oh, I don't give a damn!" he exclaimed with a wide smile.

She shook her head laughing and made one last check of her dress, seeing no signs of wear – or at least none that would be hard to explain – she picked up her mask, and cell phone that she had originally came upstairs for, and headed towards the door with Dominic. He was slipping his jacket back on, watching her intently. For a moment, they just held each other's gaze, feeling no need for words. Then Dominic grabbed Leticia by the waist, cuffed her chin with his finger and gently kissed her lips.

"Hi," he said against her mouth, his voice deep and sensual.

"Hey, Papi," Leticia greeted back, her voice low and raspy from screaming.

"Mmm, say that again," he demanded, still hovering over her lips.

"Hey, Papi," she repeated with a smile.

Dominic released another guttural groan as he sealed the moment with another kiss. Leticia could feel herself glowing as she pulled open the door to head towards the elevators. Just before she crossed the threshold into the hallway, she turned to face Dominic again, who furrowed his brow questioningly.

"Thank you for coming tonight," she said sweetly with a joyful twinkle in her eye.

"Baby, I'd cum for you any night," Dominic replied with a sneaky grin.

"Oh, my God!" she huffed with a laugh as her face went red.

Dominic gave her butt a firm pat as he closed the door behind them.

ShaRhonda L. Sharp

ShaRhonda is originally from Maywood, IL, and currently resides in Atlanta, GA.

She is a self-proclaimed "Writer-by-Passion, not by-trade," and has been published five times across various publications, including a self-published collection of poetry. She holds a Master of Written Communications degree from National Louis University in Chicago and currently works in the Telecommunications field as a means to fund the dream of being a best-selling author someday.

In between her many passion projects, she moonlights as a freelance content writer, copy editor and blogger.

Continue to follow her writing journey:

Waiting Games

by K. McCoy

Love is the one game they can't play.

Yasmine Edwards played the reality TV game show and won. She should be focused on how she wants to spend her hard-earned cash. So why does she keep thinking about the one person that she screwed over during the competition?

Xavier Sota convinced himself that he would come out on top and that was his downfall.

He saw a chance to extract his carnal brand of revenge on the assertive and full-figured Yasmine, or at least that's what he tried to tell himself.

With them both stuck at the same hotel together the day before Christmas, just what will happen next?

Will they finally allow themselves to give in to their feelings, or will the two of them end up playing themselves for the final time?

Chapter One
Wrapped Up

•• ❧ ••

All he could do was stare blankly at the television screen as Courtnee, the person he thought was going home, name was called. The modelesque brunette squealed and started twirling around with her hands stretching out to the ceiling inside her Cloudland inspired apartment. Her high-pitched voice crackled throughout his ears from the television screen, almost prompting him to turn it off.

"So, with three votes from the remaining house influencers, Xavier, you have been socially evicted." Sami Brooks, last year's winner of the competitive social experiment show, The Online Climb announced.

To get so close to the finale and be sent home fucking sucked, but that wasn't why Xavier narrowed his eyes at the screen. Just before the host told him to stand by for further instructions, he saw her picture one last time. The person he thought would at least try to help him in the competition all the way to the very end. She ain't even give him a warning, just fucking left him caught out there.

A knock was heard at the door to the apartment he was staying in, and Xavier walked to the entrance, feeling all of the previously installed cameras monitor his movements. When he opened the door, three dudes stood in front. Two had medium size cameras that they propped up over their shoulders, while the third held what looked like a large fuzzy microphone on a black pole over their heads.

"We're the exit team, here to capture your last hours in the house." the one with the fuzzy microphone explained before continuing, "And

59

to document your interaction with the house influencer you'll choose to visit before leaving."

Xavier nodded before stepping to the side of the door.

The crew members came in and positioned themselves in the living room and kitchenette area. They proceed to complain about not having enough lighting in the Creed inspired apartment and one of them detached the walkie from their hips, pressing on the side and emitting loud squawking sound inside the tiny space. Not in the mood to be around any longer than he had to, while the crew members continued to set up the scene they needed for his walk of shame, Xavier cleared his throat, "Is it cool if I head back into the bedroom for a bit? Until the Sami Books come back on?"

"Sure man."

"Cool, thanks."

He turned the corner and opened the door to what was once his bedroom. Looking around at the furnishings and hanging his head slightly, Xavier strolled past the long white dresser and mirror set in his bedroom over to the window just behind the Full XL size bed and nightstand. During the show, they weren't allowed to open the long white curtain, but now that he'd been "evicted", he figured that rule didn't apply. Reaching around the metal lamp that sat on the nightstand, he pulled back the curtain and took in the sight of snow lightly falling onto the ground. A few people were wearing light jackets with matching gloves and beanies as they crossed the street.

He thought back to the night he got on a plane from Mission, Texas to Canada months ago and after doing the math realized that Winter was just getting started. Xavier didn't have all that much experience with the cold, and he wanted to keep it that way.

On the far side of the street, a group of people were looking on as four trucks pulled into the park near a row of street lamps. Two of them had a black bucket attached to it along with a hydraulic arm. When they stopped, the men driving hopped out to walk over to the other two trucks that carried what looked like large golden bells and bushy wreaths on the back of their large truck.

Realizing what else also comes in the Winter, Xavier closed his eyes and sighed. With both his parents now gone, the only family he had left was his older brother. And the last thing he wanted to do was spend the holidays with that asshole.

"Sami Brooks is back on." one of the crew members called out.

Xavier looked out the window one last time before going back to the living room. He squinted his eyes from the bright lights that had been placed in the kitchenette, just above where the TV monitor was positioned. In his absence, another crew member now waited with the others, and he shook his head before giving the cheerful looking host his attention. Hair and makeup must be working overtime, as Sami now donned another figure-hugging dress. This one was light blue and had a slit in the front of her chest area. She also wore a pair of thin, rose gold square earrings. Her hair had been done up, with a few strands falling to the sides to frame her heart shaped face.

"Congratulations on making it this far in the game Xavier!" Sami said cheerfully. "As a previous contestant, I know all too well how hard it is to keep your wits, lies, and allies straight at this part of the journey."

He nodded, forcing himself to keep from rolling his eyes. Watching her carefully orchestrated movement on the screen, he briefly wondered just how much she was getting paid to stand around and say the shit that came out of her mouth.

"You may not be in the running for this season's top social climber, but with your eviction comes a sweet perk. You now get the chance to meet one of your former competitors still in the house." she informed him.

Next to Sami on a large whiteboard, Xavier saw the names and faces of each player in the game. Below each of the headshots, he scanned the numbers that told him which rooms each contest was in. It didn't take long for him to spot the one he wanted.

"So, who would you like to-"

"Room two." was all he said, before making his exit.

"Well, I guess he has a score to settle with Yasmine." He heard Sami nervously chuckling out loud. "The assertive technical writer and last house guest to enter the game is currently the one to beat, with Xavier now out of..."

Sami's voice faded into the background, as the crew members scurried around him to keep up with him while filming.

It didn't take long for Xavier to reach the door to the person he knew was behind him being sent home. With his hand on the doorknob, he breathed in deeply and exhaled once he turned the knob to open the door and walked in. Her suite was definitely Van Goh inspired as the plaque out front suggested above her apartment number, with its various shades of blue walls, splashes, and swirls of black, white, and gold streaks in a continuous pattern throughout the space. His footsteps were quickly absorbed into the shaggy, large dark yellow carpet while he whipped his head around looking for Yasmine.

He soon found her, wearing an all-black halter top jumpsuit in the tiny kitchen. If she heard the door open, she didn't show it. Xavier forced himself to not take another step in her direction as he studied her up close. Even with his anger fueling his next move, he couldn't help but take the moment to appreciate the view of her filling out the outfit she wore. Her stomach stuck out almost as much as her large breast did, and for a second he wondered what both would feel like in his hands. Seeing Yasmine up close, those same hands now itched to make contact over her deep golden-brown skin. But more than anything, Xavier found himself longing to see her smile.

That warm, megawatt smile that would flash across the screen whenever she won a challenge, or the smug smirk she wore when the two of them talked over the 'Top Socialites' video chat just before sending someone home. It was all he wanted to see, as a tiny part of him still refused to accept what was happening. Instead, he saw her pouring a glass from a champagne bottle in her hand. She wasn't wasting no time celebrating his eviction. Her puffy jet black locs were held back with several white strings, drawing his attention to more of her skin, along with the semicolon that was inked just behind her right ear.

When the door slammed shut from the last camera crew member entering the house, she looked up and found him staring at her, but otherwise said nothing. Xavier took a step closer to her and had to stop, as he got a whiff of warm cinnamon and pussy that wafted toward him. She extended her drink to him, and Xavier turned his head sideways in disbelief. "Did you really set me up in the last competition?" He asked as evenly as he could manage.

When she withdrew the glass from his reach and took a slow sip from it instead of answering him, Xavier narrowed his eyes at her.

"Why?"

It was her turn to cock her head sideways at him, as if the answer to his question was obvious. Yasmine sighed while shaking her head and leaving her eyes on his. "I had to."

When she turned her attention away from him and went back to pouring more champagne into the glass, he couldn't hold back anymore as he shouted, "Bullshit! You could have -"

"Lost the chance to get the Head Honcho for the week - the last week before the finale. Then it would've been me packing right now instead of you."

"I could've protected you! We had an alliance!"

The two squared off in the tiny space, all but forgetting the camera crew that was recording their heated exchange. Yasmine's smile was faint, but he saw it just before she asked in a snarky tone, "An alliance? Is that what we had?"

He jerked his head back, blinking fast as she went on, "Whatever we had is irrelevant. You want me to say that I'm sorry? Fine, I'm sorry."

"I want you to fuckin' mean it Yasmine! Don't say that shit if you don't mean it!"

"Fine!" she snapped, "Then I won't say it, cause I ain't sorry. I came here to win half a mill, not... "Xavier's eyes followed Yasmine's every movement and he watched her swallow hard before matching his glare. "...anything else."

The two stared at one another until Yasmine set her sights on the glass in her hand. She took three big gulps before turning away to sit the glass on the counter. Her shoulders slumped a bit before she whirled back around to face him. "Anything else you wanna get off your massive chest?"

His eyes widened at her cold demeanor, and he released a dark chuckle, choosing to say nothing in hopes of keeping his anger in check.

Without another word, he backed away from her and stomped away toward the front door of the apartment. Though as he reached for the knob, a soft warm hand took hold of his wrist, shocking him. Whirling around, he tried to back away from Yasmine again, but with the camera crew following her and taking up what little space was left, Xavier couldn't move more than a few inches at a time in the small foyer area. Before he could say a word, she closed the distance between them, and he was engulfed in the scent that froze him in his tracks minutes ago. The cinnamon fragrance, coupled with her signature scent, now saturated the air and was taking over the last of his good sense.

Xavier tried to focus on something - anything - that would stop his hands from itching. He felt Yasmine silently staring at him, and clinched his jaw as he lost the fight to look at her again. Seeing her ample chest rising and falling with each breath she took while glancing from his lips to his eyes was doing things to his dick that he couldn't act on in the situation they were in. But if he didn't do something soon, everyone was gonna see a print of his goods in 3D.

"What?" He growled out. "What else could you possibly want right now, Yasmine?"

He saw her set her jaw before reaching out to slide an arm around his neck. At first, he gritted his teeth but relaxed once the warmth from her hand made contact with the back of his neck. Her body was now flushed against his and Xavier instinctively licked his lips.

"I want...see if it was real."

Her lips slammed into his and immediately he gripped her full waist as close to him as he possibly could. His hands wasted no time feeling along her rolls and the small of her back. When she moaned and melted deeper into his embrace, Xavier plunged his tongue down her throat. Groaning as he tasted the semi sweetness of champagne and hints of chocolate from within her mouth, Xavier had to dig deep for enough willpower to tear himself away. When he did, he saw Yasmine's dark brown eyes and now swollen lips. Letting out a low chuckle, he reached out and roughly brushed a calloused thumb along her bottom lip.

"See you at the reunion." he whispered, backing up and opening the door to leave.

He didn't give a damn about the bright lights and shuffling of feet that were trying to keep up with him as he ripped off the mic pack from behind his lower back. As soon as he made it to his apartment, Xavier tossed the equipment onto the love seat and marched into his bedroom. Dragging out his suitcase and shoved his belongings inside, he didn't care about folding any of his clothing. Thoughts of his time on the show and competing for cash throughout the game entered his mind.

· · ⚬⟊⚬ · ·

The first week in the house was chill, as he got used to the new surroundings. He'd woken up at the end of the second week and saw on the screen that a new house guest had arrived during the night. With the final ten contestants set, they'd all be playing for their chance to win the title of "Social Climber". He heard Sami share with him and the others that her name was Yasmine, and she arrived from Florida. On his TV screen the new house guest had a bright smile and deep brown skin. And the varying shades of black and brownish red locs she had piled into two buns on her head made her look younger than the age shown at the bottom of the screen.

In the picture that went up after her headshot showed Yasmine on an elephant sanctuary trip with a group of friends, playing with elephants in the river. A baby elephant had just sprayed her with water, and she was laughing while leaning against some guy and touching another elephant's ears.

Xavier remembered staring at the picture and the ones that followed with only one question on his mind - in a competition where you could catfish until the end, why did she choose to enter the game as herself?

That was the twist of this show, since the contestants couldn't see or interact with one another outside of the cameras in their apartment or the TV screen installed, they could play the game as someone else. He already expected that that's what half of the other players were doing anyway. Xavier opted out of catfishing his way to the half a million because he didn't want to use any of his close friends' pictures to make the lies stick. Then another wild thought came to mind - maybe she *was* catfishing.

She could be pretending to be hella chubby but was really fine as hell in real life. It definitely would be something no one else had done, some kind of 'beauty is more than skin deep' type of shit.

He had nothing against fat girls, pussy was pussy in his opinion. And everyone needed cash, so he could respect the hustle. Though he didn't get any weird vibes from the chick when she finally joined the group chat. She talked like a chick and no one else seemed to be bothered by her. Maybe they all thought she'd play herself and end up going home after her first physical challenge. But when their third week inside the house had ended, Sami announced that the last evicted house guest was also the last contestant catfishing. And with that contestant no longer in the game, the house could now vote on whether or not they would get to virtually see one another for the remaining challenges. It was a round of "yeses" across the board. He was pleasantly surprised to find that Yasmine looked exactly the same as all of her pictures. Definitely heavier than any other girl he'd smashed before, but still cute.

If anything, she could be a good laugh, someone to keep him entertained for a minute. That was the plan, until he saw how competitive she was in each game the competition threw their way. Yasmine was a fighter. She could get scrappy when necessary and didn't mind playing dirty when it came to winning a challenge. He recognized the determination he saw in her instantly, as a former MMA fighter with the need and hunger to win himself.

So when she'd won Head Honcho the fourth week inside the social \experiment house, Xavier changed tactics. He decided to chat her up, maybe charm her into keeping him around for the week. What he found while messaging her privately was more than he'd imagined. Yasmine's cocky sense of humor and bluntness was unlike anything he'd come across. Usually, girls tried to impress him by pretending to be a "cool chick" or dumb down shit they knew to appease him. But he got none of those vibes from Yasmine, and it left him coming back for more.

After a month, the two were in a secret alliance and sending home anyone that became a threat. How she read people and figured out their weakness in each social and physical challenge surprised Xavier. He couldn't help but notice her body throughout the game, and Yasmine made it clear from jump that she wasn't ashamed of her fuller figure. The level of confidence she displayed while showing off her thicker form seemed to always get his dick hard.

Then things changed when he finally lost a challenge, he felt the shift in their dynamic. Though instead of using his common sense,

Xavier told himself it was just the competition getting to him. He didn't realize how true that was until it was too late.

She'd stop texting him back right away, choosing to chat it up in the morning group feed with ole blondie - the only other dude besides him still in the game. At first, he tried not to sweat it, until he lost to blondie in a physical challenge that crowned the winner to whoever held a sumo squat the longest while answering pop culture questions. With just four people left in the game, and him now in the bottom two, he knew there was a good chance he'd be sent home. That night he went into their private chat to make sure she'd do what she could to keep him in the game.

I got you.

That was all she texted him, refusing to come on the screen that night. He had no choice but to believe her words.

The voting was unanimous, and his dumb ass was left staring at the camera crew inside his studio apartment as the host announced he wouldn't be going to the finale. Now after paying her a visit, he could still smell her scent. And the shit was fucking with his head. Xavier's hands shook as he finally finished packing, with his thoughts going back to the sounds she made while in his embrace. It'd been only a minute, but he knew that if there weren't any cameras circling them, they would've gone a lot further tonight than just making out. Which was really pissing him off - since she's the reason he had to leave in the first fucking place. His entire body hummed with the need to wear hers out. To punish her for not keeping her word and not fighting to keep him in the game.

With three more weeks before the reunion, all he could do was wait. And plot his revenge.

Chapter Two
Closed Circuits

.. ⚘ ..

Yasmine stretched out in the queen-sized bed inside her suite and let out a restless sigh.

She couldn't wait to leave and start moving on now that the show had wrapped up. The production crew had offered to put all the contests up at the Falls Pointview hotel for the weekend after the reunion show taping, but everyone she talked to had opted to brave the traffic and airport crowds to try to see their families for the holidays. Since she was now three hundred thousand dollars richer, after winning second place, along with the title "The Schemist" by the online viewers during the reunion taping, the last thing Yasmine wanted was to go back home. Her family wasn't good for much, but she knew they would be lined up to see her once the news broke about her winnings. Each one of them with their hands out to try and guilt or hustle her out of whatever funds they could. So, she was more than cool with spending Saint Nick's workday at a hotel on the show's dime.

Though after getting word from production minutes ago, Yasmine learned that she wasn't the only contestant that decided to stay in Canada like she'd thought.

While being taken to her new digs by one of the production assistants, she overheard on the walkies that Xavier didn't book a flight with the others. The minute she heard his name, Yasmine resigned herself to staying in her room - until her New Year's Eve flight if she had to. Flashes of how he glared at her during the reunion were still at the

69

front of her mind. He made the whole day of taping draining as hell for her. From choosing to sit directly behind her, murmuring under his breath but loud enough for the mics to pick up about how he'd helped her earn "The Schemist" title and felt that half of the fifty grand should be his, to him provoking Sami to ask as many questions as he could that hinted at their alliance just so he could tell everyone how betrayed he was by her changing things up to get to the final three.

All she wanted now was to avoid his salty ass, especially now that the cameras weren't on them anymore. At least, that's what she tried to tell herself she wanted. But just like the night he left; she couldn't stop imagining kissing him. Ever since the two of them first chatted privately in the house chat while on the show, she felt a pull to him. She didn't know why he messaged her that day, but after he did, the game changed. They started working together, blindsiding the competition. Yasmine always had a huge competitive streak, and with Xavier's athleticism and her strategic skills, they had no trouble making sure to be the last ones standing. If she was honest with herself, the shit turned her on.

Which is exactly why she had to get rid of him.

Once it was down to the final four, Yasmine knew that was the best time to get him out of the game. He'd started messaging her relentlessly in their private chats after the fifth contestant got evicted, telling her how he'd 'be honored' to be her knight in shining armor when the time came.

I got you Yasi.

Seeing that message gave Yasmine all the resolve she needed to go through with her new plan. She hit up the other two players in a new private group chat and proposed making alliances with them, promising to send Xavier home, and securing their spots to the semifinals. As long as one of them went into the bottom two with him, they each had her word that she wouldn't vote them out. And she held up on her end of the new deal, which got her to the finals.

Yasmine knew that Xavier was going to come to her studio apartment as soon as he was eliminated, and Yasmine tried to be cool when he burst through the door. But watching him turn away to walk out the door left her yearning for something she hadn't wanted from another person in years. Sex was one thing, but whatever the growing connection was that she was beginning to feel for Xavier over the last few weeks had her feet following him before she could stop herself. Thinking back to their kiss, Yasmine found herself bolting up from the bed, warm all over.

"I need a drink." Yasmine blurted out in the empty room.

Slipping on a pair of brown suede boots and grabbing her small gold chain purse, she made her way out of the room and onto the nearest elevator. After stepping out, she read the directory posted on the wall and walked across the hotel lobby. She shivered as a strong wind gathered and whipped around the long jersey knit wrap around canary yellow dress she wore from someone exiting the hotel's automatic sliding doors. Smooth jazz music could be heard the further she ventured down the carpeted hall. Soon the clinking of glasses and light laughter reached her ears as she spotted a few patrons enjoying themselves around the bar.

Its interior was mostly graphite and silver hues, a stark difference from the rest of the hotel, which seemed to have more of a mountainous style to it. The wall nearest to her had floor to wall windows that allowed Yasmine to see that it was still snowing heavily outside. A grand Pine Fir tree that almost reached the ceiling was decorated in silver bells, matching ornaments, and at least a thousand twinkling white tealights. She stared at the large star that hung at the top and wondered briefly how long it took the staff to get such a beautiful display completed in time for guests to marvel at for the holidays. To her right, several black and gray panels lined the wall.

Water gently flowed from each one, complimenting the music that followed throughout the area. While looking for an empty seat at the bar, she found one. It just happened to be right next to the person she'd planned on staying away from for the week.

She watched Xavier from behind, slowly sipping on a dark drink, before taking two gulps and setting down the glass. His face was twisted in a scowl for a second as he waved over the bartender, who went about refreshing his drink. Yasmine remembered seeing in pictures from his package video during the finale special that he liked to drink with friends back home. So she shouldn't have been surprised to find him down here knocking back a few rounds.

After leaving the game, he started growing out his beard. While in the competition, it was always kept in a neatly trimmed goatee. But by the time they taped for the finale and reunion, that goatee had become an impressive full beard that stretched and connected with his trimmed sideburns. One that she would sneak peeks at during their breaks while taping. Now that she had time away from his ornery behavior on set, she could really observe him.

Even from a distance, Yasmine had to admit that Xavier Sota exuded sex appeal. He stared at himself in the mirror behind the bar, brooding while occasionally drifting over to look out the window closest to him. The brown loafers he wore almost touched the floor from the barstool he sat comfortably in, hinting at his five-foot-nine frame. She took in more of his appearance, allowing herself to drink in his husky build within the dark crimson sweater and brown slacks he donned. As his hand with the drink in it went midair, she saw the faint vein lines in his knuckles before getting distracted by his inviting lips. Yasmine remembered all too well how soft yet firm those lips were when they were pressed against hers.

After spending all day yesterday avoiding him, she wondered for a second if she should go up to him. Though just as she was about to, four women stumbled in from the lobby and beat her to it. Dressed in their barely there attire of sheer tops, short skirts and dresses, Yasmine knew they'd just gotten back from clubbing as the women swarmed the bar. And without missing a beat, two of them batted their eyelashes and grinned wide in front of Xavier. Seeing him nod at them, Yasmine's chest tightened as she gripped the chain on her purse. She didn't want to be jealous, hell, she didn't have a right to be. But the feeling continued to make itself at home in her chest, sprouting out to the crown of her head as she zeroed in on one of the ladies casually running her arm up and down Xavier's solid forearm while sitting in the seat next to him.

"Daaaammmnnn Santa baby!" she slurred out, giggling while leaning against her friend.

She watched as the two taller women in the small entourage sashayed and flanked Xavier, both grinning like Christmas had arrived early as they openly and lasciviously stared at him.

"You wanna get naughty with us tonight?" the one with ash blonde hair and the sparkly rose gold dress purred, making sure to brush her petite breast along Xavier's shoulder.

Her friend, sporting a ginger pixie cut and the sheerest halter top Yasmine had ever seen, was not to be outdone, as she lazily trailed her dainty fingers down his chest and puckered up her shimmery parchment lips in his direction. Yasmine gritted her teeth when Xavier leaned in to say something to the woman in the dress. Though when he pulled away, the blonde gawked at him.

"Your loss, Hulk."

The women that chose to share the last available seat together at the bar must have thought what she said was funny as they burst out laughing while blondie wobbled back over to them. Still not ready to give up just yet, the one with the pixie cut eyed him slowly while making her lips disappear by bringing them inward. "C'mon big man, let me jingle your balls tonight." she brazenly brought a hand to his thigh." I promise to make it worth your while."

Yasmine swallowed hard as she looked on at the exchange in front of her, with Xavier looking down at the pixie girl's tiny hand resting on his solid thigh. When he finally stood and went over to the bartender on the other side of the bar, the jealousy she felt turned into something else entirely. That feeling began to blossom as she looked on at Xavier, who was leaning over the bar counter, signing a receipt. Her eyes followed him while he strolled down the hall and away from her as she remained hidden against the mirrored wall. Once he passed her, Yasmine's feet soon went in the same direction. Making sure to keep a good distance between them, she felt her heart pick up speed as fewer and fewer people were seen in the hallway.

"Yasmine."

She froze at the sound of her name. Whipping her eyes from side to side, Yasmine quickly realized her mistake – the columns placed straight down the hallway were also reflective, making it easy to see whoever was behind you at all times. With nowhere to run, Yasmine took a deep breath as Xavier turned around and locked eyes with her. She wanted to move but couldn't, lost in the storm that brewed behind his amber eyes. He marched up to her and didn't ask for permission as he grabbed her hand. Xavier didn't let go, even as Yasmine slightly winced. Walking quickly to avoid tripping from trying to keep up behind him, she found herself bumping into his back as they stood in front of the elevator.

When it finally opened, he pressed a button while yanking her to his side. Though just as the doors were about to close, a group of guys tried to get on with them."Take the next one." Xavier barked out, stepping closer to the elevator doors and blocking them from entering.

She didn't get a chance to try and say anything once the sliding doors closed, as Xavier whirled around quickly and firmly pressed her against one of the mirrored walls inside.

"You like watching me now?" Xavier asked, his voice dangerously low.

He pinned her hands behind her back and Yasmine's heartbeat spiked from getting a whiff of the sweet yet spicy liquor on his breath.

Leaning in close, his breath fanned the back of Yasmine's neck as he spoke again. "Was it worth it?"

She heard the strained tone in his voice and found herself wanting to soothe it away. Looking directly at him and seeing the intense glare on his face, Yasmine felt an all too familiar heat began to radiate in between her legs. Soon she struggled to make out his face as condensation buildup on the mirror in front of her.

"Since you got your cash, was it worth it? Fucking me over?"

With the sensations of his voice and touch overriding her ability to think clearly, Yasmine tried desperately to say something. But she wasn't quick enough. Xavier's free hand palmed her ass while he began pulling up the fabric of her dress. A cool breeze teased her cheeks before spreading to her growing hot pussy. Her eyes widened when Xavier reached for the left side of her panties, hastily pulling and snapping the elastic against her skin. She gasped while he continued exploring more of her full form, skimming his hands down from her hip and thigh. Hearing him inhale, her heart hammered hard against her chest.

"From the smell in here right now, I'll take that as a yes."

She gasped again when he brought himself closer, rubbing the front of his slacks against her ass. The friction of his hardness through the fabric left her fighting to keep her eyes open.

"I should fuck you right here. Consider it my consolation prize."

"Xav-..."

He rendered her speechless once more when his hand roamed further down the lower half of her warm body. Her arousal had begun to trickle its way down to her mid inner thighs and he let out a dark chuckle.

"Yeah, I bet you'd fuckin' like that, uh?" She bit the corner of her lip to hold back a moan when Xavier nipped on her earlobe. "This ain't a bad parting gift you got for me, but I bet you can do better."

Yasmine knew that she should stop him from going any further while they were inside this elevator. But as she felt his hand inching toward her moist center, Yasmine didn't care to. The last thought that entered her mind was whether or not he'd press the emergency button in time.

Just before he could get more of a feel of the effect he was having on her, the elevator came to a stop. Her stomach dropped as the dinging sound made it to her ears. Feeling the absence of Xavier's warmth, Yasmine turned around in time to see him take her hand. They wordlessly walked out of the elevator.

Chapter Three
The Reunion

. . ⚘ . .

Yasmine said nothing as they stood in front of the door to his room. She looked on as Xavier leaned his head against the front door before finally speaking.

"If you don't want this, say so now."

He didn't turn around as his grip on her hand tightened, but she chose to remain silent.

"Yasi...you already played me once. Before we go any further, you gotta say that shit out loud. "

Again, the pain she heard in his voice made her chest ache. Ever since kissing him the night he left The Online Climb, Xavier was never too far from her mind. And even if she didn't realize it earlier, subconsciously she wanted to run into him tonight. She wanted to know if what she was feeling for him in the competition was real. The night she'd kissed him, she knew.

"I need to hear you say it."

As evenly as she possibly could, Yasmine answered him, "Yeah, I want this."

Muffled voices throughout the hotel filled the empty space around them before he took out his key card. Once the beeping ended and the door opened, Xavier stepped inside and turned to look at her. His eyes blazed with desire as he took his time glancing at her from head to toe. This time both her core and heart thumped, almost in unison as she took the first step inside.

77

Walking into his hotel room, Yasmine placed her purse on the black marble top of the dresser next to the small Christmas tree that matched the one inside her suite. She slipped off her boots before glancing over her shoulder and found him still staring at her. She could've sworn that Xavier's deep amber irises were swirling as she watched him. The sight left her fully aware of their intent - to seek and destroy. Knowing that didn't scare her. In fact, that was precisely what the small voice inside her head wanted. Ever since that night, when she saw him for the first time in person, Yasmine knew it would come to this. And she wanted to be sought out and devoured by him.

She heard the loud click of the door closing just as Xavier's breath suddenly ghosted across her right earlobe. Yasmine's core pulsed rapidly when she felt his lips brush lightly against her ear.

"You still not sorry? For how you played me?"

She thought back to the reunion interview and how she played mental gymnastics to avoid answering this very question. Now with no cameras or an audience, she was left to tell the truth.

"I didn't trust you then. I-I couldn't."

"Why? Why didn't you trust me?"

"It was a game, Xavier. And even though I felt... bad about what I decided to do, I couldn't bring myself to trust you or your words."

"So, to avoid getting played, you played me?"

"I played the game!"

His hand was around her throat in seconds. "Yeah, you did sweet tart. You played the game. And almost won too. Now we're here... "

Her brows scrunched up at the moniker he used, but before she could question him about it, Yasmine felt his grip around her throat tighten.

"I wanna see just how sorry you are."

The dim lights within the room came to her mind in little snapshots as she fought to keep them open. But Xavier was making that more and more difficult to do with each passing second, as his other hand roamed along the sides of her dress. Bringing her thighs together, he squeezed her left ass cheek, then the right one, and let out a deep groan. His calloused hands rubbed her backside, just before pulling up the fabric to her dress. As a brief coolness reached her exposed thighs and ass for the second time, Yasmine almost didn't hear the tearing of her panties.

Though instead of letting the ruined undergarments fall to the ground, he slowly twisted and pulled them back toward him, making sure the material teased her slick folds every inch of the way. Jerking and almost losing her balance during his taunting game of tug of war, Yasmine panted in relief once he completely removed the panties.

"Yeah, I kind of believe you now."

"I am!" Yasmine defiantly shouted.

"So you say. Let's see what else you can do when properly motivated."

She tried to quench a little bit of her desire by rubbing her thighs closer together, but Xavier immediately put an end to that with a sound smack to her ass check.

"Ahhh! Mhhmmm..."

Her voice didn't even sound like her own as he cupped and caressed a hand slowly along the stinging area. The unique pain and pleasure he brought to her highly sensitive skin was almost more than she could stand.

"You don't move without my say so. Understand?" Xavier told her, removing his hand from her ass.

"Y-yes."

It'd been over a year since she'd let anyone touch her, and Yasmine wasn't sure how much longer she would last before turning into a passionate puddle from his sensual yet rough ministrations.

"Good. Now take this off," he commanded.

Yasmine started to face him, but he stopped her. "Wha-"

"You think you can handle what I'll do if you don't follow my instructions?" Xavier warned.

Her body involuntarily shuddered from the images her mind conjured up of how he'd back up his threat before she bent over, collecting the ends of the dress in her hands.

Xavier brought her soaked panties to his nose and deeply inhaled while he watched Yasmine do what he'd asked. Her tangy yet sweet scent from in the elevator minutes ago was all he could think about, fucking up all his good sense. Seeing her from behind, gathering the dress into her hands and lifting it over her head, Xavier sunk his teeth into his bottom lip before shoving her undergarments into the pocket of his slacks. All she had left on was a bra, with its ends snugly folded into one of her thick back rolls. His eyes caught sight of another one of her tattoos - eight small etchings of the moon cycle, that went vertically down her spine, stopping just before the space where most people would normally get inked on their lower back. After enjoying the view of her ass, he realized that the clasp to her bra was in the front instead of the back as he'd expected. Stepping forward, Xavier gently placed his hands along the straps as he pulled them down. Goosebumps appeared on her arms, further prompting him to wrap his around her heaving chest.

As much as he wanted her to feel his frustration about the choice she made, Xavier found himself wanting to make this time between them last for as long as he could. Because once she left this room, she wouldn't have another reason to ever see him again.

Letting her go, Xavier reached down to the front of her chest and unclasped the bralette she wore, freeing her breasts. He got lost in the sight of each swaying motion that followed as her nipples proudly stood at attention. Blinking his eyes and reminding himself to focus, Xavier let his hands begin a slow exploration of her body, cupping as much as he could of one of her heavy breasts in his hands.

Using both of his hands, he kneaded them together and bit down on his lips as Yasmine leaned back to rest her head on his shoulders. When she purred, his dick thumped in anticipation against her ass. Releasing her breasts, he made his way past her side rolls. His nails lightly trailed along the sides of her hips, before grabbing her soft stomach.

Listening to her moans grow louder, Xavier brought his mouth down to the space where her neck and shoulder met and suckled firmly. She trembled in his arms. While seeing the effect he was having on her - without being inside of her yet - it removed the lingering doubt that he had about being capable of pleasing her. Excitement built in his chest about getting to learn what other things he could do to make her squirm. Xavier greedily applied more pressure to her exposed skin. As he pulled his lips away with a smack and glanced down at the first passion mark he left on her body, his hands went lower, soundly lifting her stomach before they both groaned at the same time from his fingertips grazing over her warm mound. Sweeping his hand across the plush skin, he quickly stopped and curled his fingers further below to feel her dampness.

"X-Xavier...fuck me."

That was what he'd missed about her the most over the last month - the bluntness Xavier came to crave when talking with her. Though he also relished the sound of wanting in Yasmine's voice as she begged him to fuck her. Hearing her moan was the best gift ever and he wanted to savor every second. But first he had a few more questions. He knew she would fight him every step of the way before giving in and answering him. In his wicked mind, he thought of it as mere foreplay and was counting on it. If she remained true to form like she was during the show, Yasmine was not going to go down without trying.

"Did I give you a reason to not trust me? Ever?" Xavier asked, using his free hand to bring one of her stiff nipples together with his thumb and index finger.

She was already taking in shallow breaths, so when he pinched the dark brown pebble in his hands, he couldn't help turning his lips upward to the sound of her moans. His dick jerked in his slacks when Yasmine's ass grinded against him. Gritting his teeth, Xavier brought his hand from the front of her heated core and took a step back. With his other hand remaining on her breast, he squeezed harder.

Yasmine shook her head and tightly shut her eyes. "No," she breathed out.

"When did you decide to set me up?"

Letting go of her nipple, Xavier looked on as she hung her head and breathed heavily. He knew she was trying to keep it together but seeing her practically naked in front of him, he was more determined than ever to make her fall apart. "Answer me Yasi. When did you decide I had to go?"

He pushed a knee between her legs and chuckled as she swayed. Dropping to his knees, Xavier inhaled the scent of her arousal and immediately gripped his dick through his slacks. He placed a kiss on the back of each of her knees, working his way up to her thighs. When the first taste of her nectar hit his tongue, Xavier groaned. "Yeah, sweet tart. That's the perfect name for you."

Her essence reminded him of something sweet and tart, like Agua fresca de Jamaica that he loved to drink back home before moving to the States. He rushed out of his slacks and briefs in between lapping up more of her juices from the inside of each of her thighs. Once his dick was free, Xavier gripped the base and stroked the full thick length of himself, briefly closing his eyes. He could feel the precum coating his hands as he inched closer to Yasmine's core. Her thighs shook slightly as he smacked and snacked on her heady goodness and Xavier wanted to drink from her until he got full. Though as much as he wanted to keep tasting and teasing her, he knew she'd come soon if he did. Biting the inside of his cheeks, Xavier lowered his head, forcing himself to not dive back into her sweetness. He was rewarded for his efforts the minute he stopped.

"Shit! Wh...when y-y-you said...you- you got me." she panted out. "In the chat."

He saw her legs shaking softly and went to work on marking the back of her left thigh near her ass cheek. Holding on to her thigh with both hands, he suckled hard on her skin as her moans filled the room. He could hear her pants when he finally stopped long enough to admire his handiwork. A vibrant reddish-purple bruise about the size of his index finger and thumb appeared on her brown skin. He quickly looked up and found Yasmine holding both of her breasts in each hand, squeezing them together.

"Why?" he questioned again. "Why didn't you take a chance and trust me?"

She said nothing, choosing in vain to try to create friction between her legs. Luckily, he was kneeling in front of her, and Xavier quickly brought a hand to her pussy and cupped it roughly.

"Ahhh! Please! I was so close..." Yasmine whined.

"I swear - I'll leave you withering for release where you stand if you don't answer me." he declared sharply before asking again, "Why couldn't you just fuckin' trust me?"

"I didn't do it because I didn't trust you! I did it because I was starting to!"

Xavier paused as he looked up at her, his eyes wide as he watched her closely.

"You were distracting me! Telling me all that shit in the chat, how you'd protect me, how you had my back." Yasmine let go of her breast and he let his hand fall to the side as she continued, "I wanted to believe you - that made you a threat. So I had to get rid of you!"

Hearing her once rebellious and stubborn voice now edged on the verge of tears, Xavier couldn't not believe her. But if what she's saying is the truth, then that meant...

"You wanted to believe me?" he repeated before the truth came out of his mouth, "Then...you...you wanted me too back then? When you first kissed me?"

He didn't give her a chance to answer as he stood and kicked his slacks completely off. When he was in front of Yasmine, she immediately reached for the front of his sweater, bringing his face closer. He pulled himself away and quickly brought the sweater over his head and tossed it across the room. Their eyes locked onto one another, and he couldn't resist extending a hand out to touch her cheek. She leaned toward his hand and brushed her lips against his fingertips, nipping at the tips and causing him to breathe heavily.

Xavier knew what he was about to say could change what was about to go down, but he had to know. He had to ask her before he got balls deep inside her. "Yasi, say this is more than just a fuck."

Instead of saying anything, she went in for a kiss, but Xavier pulled away. "I wanna hear you say it."

Keeping his eyes on her, he could see hers dart around the room. But when Yasmine's gaze landed back onto him, Xavier didn't miss how they softened while her chest rose again.

"I can see it, Yasi. The same way I feel, I see it in your eyes right now."

"Then why you need me to say anything?"

"Because...I just fuckin' do! So stop tryin' to front and say -"

"I have feelings for you!" Yasmine blurted out, "Damn! Is that what you want to hear?"

Closing the space between them, Xavier grabbed the back of her head. "Yeah."

His lips crushed hers, trapping her moans as he dipped her backwards. Their bodies molded together, with his dick sticking to one of her thighs. When his hands went to grab her ass, Yasmine wrapped her hands around his neck and he scooped her up, breaking away from her eager kisses just long enough to deeply inhale her strong arousal that penetrated the air. With her legs around his thick waist, the two of them waddled to the edge of the bed before he got lost in the feel of her tongue massaging his.

When he sat her down at the foot of the queen-sized bed, Yasmine immediately reached for his dick, but he swatted her hand away. His whole body vibrated as she held his stare. Soon her hands were in between her legs and the gushing sounds she made while stroking herself was making him dumb as fuck. Needing to give her something else to do before he got off on the sight in front of him, Xavier harshly commanded. "Wrap your hands around my dick."

She reached out a hand and just as he thought she was going to do what he said, Yasmine wet her lips and craned her neck forward. He went crossed eyed at the sight of her pretty pink tongue collecting his precum.

"Ugh! Damn Yasi..." he choked out.

His hand immediately went to the back of her head, allowing him to tangle his fingers into her fluffy yet thick twists. Closing his eyes, Xavier briefly imagined he was gathering clouds with his bare hands and that sent his mind into orbit. Soon his thoughts floated between his two mother tongues, with more truths ready to spill from his lips. Xavier released a low growl as more of his dick disappeared inside her mouth. When she moaned and relaxed her jaw, allowing room for all of him to fit inside, he sputtered out in Spanish. "Ay, ay, ay, nin-fa..."

Pumping himself in and out of her warm mouth, he was left gasping for air when Yasmine sucked harder, coating his balls with her sticky essence while she fondled them in her hands. He could feel himself about to release down her throat, and as much as he wanted to, he couldn't. Letting go of the back of her head, he staggered backward and his hunger for her grew at the sight of saliva that stretched from her bottom lip to the tip of his hardness.

"I was just getting started." Yasmine said seductively, using her thumb and index finger to wipe the moisture from the corners of her mouth. He watched as her eyes roamed over his tattooed chest and down to his throbbing dick again before adding, "Guess it's true what they say."

Clearing the wet dream of her naked and his pre-cum on her chin out of his mind, Xavier kept his voice even when he asked, "What's that?"

"It's better with feelings involved."

He stalked toward her and lifted her chin. Seeing the megawatt smile he fell for during their time together on the show, Xavier's heart glided fast to the middle of his throat. Without a word he leaned down and placed a peck to her lips. Feeling her smile, he swiped his tongue along the seam of her lips, parting them before diving in. While bringing the rest of his body closer to hers, he grabbed one of her breasts before colliding with her. She immediately wrapped her legs around him before falling onto her back. Seeing her underneath him, waiting for him, he slowly reached between them and aligned his dick to her slick center.

A stream of mewls left her mouth as he teased her, brushing up and down her pussy. Just as she opened her mouth, he swiftly filled her to the hilt. He knew being inside her sweet heat would feel incredible, but it felt better than he ever imagined. The way Yasmine's warmness wrapped around him, her snug sweetness had him ready to let go of everything that went down on the show. Hell, he was almost ready to do that anyway, but being in her love's embrace now sealed his fate.

She gripped his waist, digging her nails into his sides. Gritting his teeth, he willed himself to stay still so he could study her face. Until she began to grind against him, moving her hands from his lower back to his shoulders. Her scent was now everywhere, enveloping him, all the while coaxing him to drag himself through her rippled waves of paradise and plunge back in.

"Ah! Xavier, that's it!" Yasmine cried out, "Give it to me!"

Again and again, their bodies said what they wouldn't out loud, slapping together almost in sync until he slipped his hand down and gently applied pressure to her clit with his thumb. He felt her arch closer to his chest while he steadily swiped left and right onto her love button. Her chest glistened with sweat, and he thought she never looked more fucking beautiful than she did at that moment.

"Xavier! Fuck - you gonna make me come!" she whined.

As much as he wanted to make her tap out, Xavier wasn't done yet. With each stroke, he fought to leave her warmth, even after figuring out just how he wanted her to come on his dick. Deciding to countdown to three, once he dove inside her pussy on the last count, he willed himself to stay still.

"No." he grunted out.

Removing his thumb from her swollen clit, he slipped out of her completely. Her frustrated groans made their way to his ears, and he tuned them out as he grabbed a pillow from over her head. Choosing his words carefully in English, Xavier requested with a ragged breath, "Turn over."

Her eyes grew twice their size, and he pressed a chaste kiss to her shoulder while pleading silently with his for her to continue to trust him. Letting out a breath he wasn't aware he was holding, Xavier watched as she slowly did what he asked. With her back now facing him, he placed the pillow under her lower stomach and placed more kisses down along her spine.

"Lay down."

Yasmine eased onto the pillow and as she turned her head to look back at him, seeing her bite down on her bottom lip in anticipation sent his hands down to his dick. Kneeling behind her while stroking himself, he groaned at the way the Christmas lights flickered and cast a prism of reds, greens, and yellows over her lush figure. Starting with the heels of her feet, Xavier crouched low and went to work planting wet kisses all over her body.

"Ohhh, mmmhhh, Xavier... "she breathed out.

He made sure to pay special attention to the back of her knees and her thighs, after hearing more of her deep sighs when he lingered along those spots. Before long she had finally relaxed enough for him to nestle in between her legs. Placing a tender kiss to her right shoulder blade, Xavier positioned himself at Yasmine's dripping pussy. Inching back inside her sweetness, he took his time, allowing them both to enjoy the feel of his dick stretching and accommodating itself inside her tight walls. He couldn't hold back the mixture of Spanish and English that began spilling from his mouth."Damn Yasi, dulzura...no, mi alma..."

He didn't know if she understood anything he was saying, but even if Xavier wanted to, he couldn't stop the words from leaving his mouth. With each stroke he found himself getting more and more lost inside her warmth. Wrapping her tighter into his arms, he lifted himself up a little higher to increase the rhythmic pounding of his strokes. "You can have it all. The money ain't it for me, not anymore. Mi gordita - mi alma..." he whispered along the shell of her ear.

"Xavier...please...ah!" She tried in vain to escape his hold by grasping at the bed sheets, but he refused to let her go.

Slowing down their tantalizing tempo, Xavier gently bit onto her earlobe before flicking out his tongue to sample the sweat that had collected on her neck. Yasmine's hands shook as she outstretched them again, making another attempt to get away by clawing at the bed sheets before finally slapping her hands hard against the mattress.

"FU-CK! You gonna make me come...please let me - please!" she pleaded.

Yasmine threw her head back toward him, and Xavier nuzzled along her chin before kissing her cheek.

"Ay, ay, I'm through fightin' you - te necestio...te necesito, mi gordita... te necesito."

Her jet black and auburn twists spilled out across her back and shoulders, so he swept them to the side while peppering more kisses onto her skin. Bucking her hips while underneath him, a crescendo of whimpers escaped her lips just as her walls clamped down around him.

"Yes! Oh yes! I-I'm coming!" she cried out in ecstasy.

He tried to fight the tightening of his balls but quickly lost as spasm after spasm left his entire body trembling when he filled her. "Yasi!"

The room grew quiet, apart from their heavy breathing and the whirl of snowflakes whipping against the windows. After catching his breath, Xavier wordlessly left the bed and made his way to the bathroom. He grabbed a clean towel and ran warm water over it before going back to Yasmine, who had propped herself up onto the pillows. Quietly, he wiped her down and returned to the bathroom. Though as he was returning to bed after freshening up, Xavier came to an abrupt stop at the sight of Yasmine in front of him. Brushing her breast along his solid chest, she leaned the rest of her body against his.

"Next round, I'm taking charge."

He couldn't help but chuckle, placing a chaste kiss to her forehead. "We'll see, sweet tart."

A smirk spread across her face before she tilted upward and captured his lips with her own. It wasn't rushed like the ones before it, so he made sure to enjoy every stroke of her tongue while it mingled with his until she placed a hand on his chest.

"We got all weekend, Xavier. Don't make me wear your ass out."

His eyes swept over the rest of her ample physique and thoughts of teasing and tussling with her well into Christmas day instantly made his dick hard again. Sighing as he brought her into his embrace, Xavier couldn't think of a more blissful way to spend the holiday than with the woman who he was fiercely falling for - Yasmine Edwards.

K. McCoy is the author of the novel *A Dove's Cry*.

Through indie author webinars, she helps authors write drama filled, heart gripping, and authentic stories. In her many years of publishing, she has traveled around the world, crafting stories based on real-world experiences, combined with hopeful possibilities. As a serial hobbyist, you can find her studying other languages, tinkering with her camera, or trying out a new Yoga pose when she's not writing or working on another bittersweet story.

For more on K. McCoy's future works, in-person events, and monthly sweet excerpts, please join The Stories Station[1], or visit her website atwww.authorkmccoy.com[2].

---

1.   https://krealmccoy.ck.page/a3846a397d

2.   http://www.authorkmccoy.com

The Perfect Snow Globe

by E.A. Noble

"He wanted Emily, needed to have her, be near her, and if the choice was to lose her or force himself into her perfect snow globe of a world then he would grit his teeth and do so, even if it hurt. Luckily, he liked pain and torture."

In a post-apocalyptic world overrun by superhuman glitches, Jack and Emily's love is put to the ultimate test. As they fight for survival against the relentless hordes, they must also confront the fractures in their own relationship. When Emily is abducted, Jack embarks on a dangerous journey to get her back, discovering the true power of their love amidst dangerous foes. Will they defy the odds and find solace in each other's arms, or will the darkness of their world tear them apart forever?

• • ⁓ • •

Warnings:

Murder; Kidnapping; Blood; Rough Sex

Act 1

The rotten smell of decaying flesh wafted through the cracked glass on the second floor of the abandoned Christmas Palace. Jack adjusted his respiratory mask as he peered out of the window watching two glitches below. The zombie-like creatures had silver metallic pus running out of their ears, nose, and blackened mouths as they ripped through captured white rats with red bitty eyes. The snarls of the glitches and squeaks of the rats could be heard for miles, due to this entire town being one of the first to fall when humanity died.

"Fuck this shit." Jack sneered as the glitches finished eating the rats and began attacking each other. He leaned back from the window, careful not to make any noise that would gain attention from the barely living monsters below. Jack wished these were zombies, that every ounce of their humanity had died when they turned, at least, they would be easier to kill. But unfortunately, deep down in their infected little brains was still life, not one worth living though.

Cautiously, he turned to make his way down the overturned aisles filled with broken Christmas lights, crumpled holiday cards, and scattered Christmas decorations. The fluorescent lights flickered above casting shadows on the shelves with cracked ornaments, torn stockings, and remnants of a holiday long gone. Jack spotted his wife, Emily, shifting through the rubble like this was a Trader Joe's pre-apocalypse.

"Spotted two glitches. We need to move." Jack checked his suctioned ear covers and goggles to make sure his protective gear was secured. The last thing any of them needed was a bite. He slid his hands over his double layered black combat suit. It was reinforced to protect against the silver poison that spilled from the glitches' mouths.

96

Emily reached down and pulled back a red shopping cart. "We can go after I find what I'm looking for." The moment the cart left its spot, a music box clicked on playing a broken toon of the Christmas Fairy.

Jack and Emily stared at the music box as if it were a novelty only seen rarely. Honestly, in today's climate, it might just have been. Jack tightened his grip on his standard issue 9mm, his eyes shot back toward the cracked window facing the alley.

"Shut that thing up," He whispered.

Emily bent over, attempting to look for the off switch. "I don't see how to turn it off."

Snarls grew louder on the outside.

More were coming. Jack switched his hand from his 9mm to the Mossberg 500 Cruiser strapped to his back. He strained to listen, but the ally went silent. Losing patience, Jack marched over and gave the faded red and green box a kick. It puttered then the tune slowly dragged before shutting completely down. The couple waited, standing in place, their ears searching for the slightest bit of movement within the long-forgotten store. Hearing none, they let out a breath.

Emily rubbed her gloved hands together then kicked a pile of Christmas junk with her leather boots. "I'm going to search over there. I mean, when the world went to shit, did it take all the snow globes with it?" She said, her voice muffled by her own mask. "You know," she pushed a few more baskets out of her way. "This search would go a lot faster if you helped."

Jack re-strapped his Cruiser and sighed deeply. "What's the point of gathering Christmas supplies to celebrate tomorrow?" He grumbled; his heavy breaths hit the back of his mask. "Everyone we know is dead. The world ended months ago."

Emily shot him a glare. "It's not just about the world, Jack. This is the first Christmas when we won't have friends and family. I think now is the perfect time to remember them and celebrate."

Jack snuck over to another window. He peered down into the alley. There were no glitches in sight. "Where did you fuckers go?" He tapped a finger on his gun handle and scanned the abandoned buildings looking for signs of where they could have gone.

Emily continued speaking as she yanked a shelf upright. "Plus, it's about us. Our love. Our memories. Christmas was always special to me, and I refuse to let some outbreak take that away."

"So, you rather risk our lives to search for a snow globe?" Jack threw a glance over his shoulder.

"Not just any snow globe, but a Victorian vintage snow globe. My parents had one just like it when I was young. It had the perfect little house, surrounded by snow covered trees, with a little cute red carriage out front, with kids building a chubby little snowman." Emily's voice became strained behind the mask. "And before all of this..." She gestured to the raided store with its broken shelves and bullet riddled walls. "...this was the only store that sold them."

Jack clicked his teeth and eased his fingers off of the gun handle. He knew deep down that Emily was looking for a distraction, a way to feel normal in a not so normal world, but was this the hill she simply had to die on? The only reason he agreed to come on this venture was because this town was far away from the city Chimango, where the first outbreak took place. This area was supposed to be cleared out months ago, but that was a lie.

"We're losing the sun." Jack turned his gaze to the polluted orange filled sky. "We can try again next Christmas. You always wanted to go to Winterland, right? It's not too far from here. Maybe we can do that instead."

Emily froze. "I know what you're trying to do, and I appreciate it. I truly do." She glanced across the store with sadden eyes. "But I need this, Jack. I need—" She began searching the aisles, more vigorously this time. "To feel like me again, like us. The way we used to be before the outbreak. When the people we love weren't all—" her voice drifted.

It had been eight in a half months since the fallout. Jack watched his best friend being ripped to pieces by the first silvered-eyed glitch. The memory haunted Jack every time he shut his eyes at night. Dead, all of them, dead.

Emily gasped. "Eureka!" She jumped over a stack of old dried reeds and an overturned decaying Christmas tree. As she dived in between two counters, her boots swung in the air like a kid in a toy bin. She came back up with a crumbled box. With a shaking hand, she carefully peeled back the box until it revealed a mint condition snow globe—a delicate sphere encasing a beautiful white Christmas.

Jack could sense a bittersweet smile tugged at her lips behind the mask as she cradled the snow globe in her hands. "I found it," her voice trembled. "This...this is what I needed."

Jack's gaze softened as he watched Emily hug the globe to her chest. He gave her a minute before clearing his throat. "Can we go now?"

She nodded, tucking the globe into her leather pouch and securing the bag on her shoulders. The couple eased their way to the first floor of the store and down a forever frozen escalator. The rusted metal bloomed with dirt and silver metallic fungus that in appearance, looked much like a snow eared mushroom. These blooming fungi were due to the silver blood that spilled from the glitches. If not properly cleaned, they grow like weeds, drowning everything they touch. Luckily, it wasn't poisonous when it was in this form. The disease could only be spread when it's in contact with the blood steam.

When they reached the bottom of the stairs, a snarl echoed out in the lobby. Jack stretched an arm over Emily's chest to halt her where she stood. Another snarl, to the left this time, then another behind them. Out of the dimly lit shelves, silver-eyed glitches appeared. Crimson staining their mouths.

These creatures were fast, but clumsy. Driven by their need to feed; they would walk until their feet no longer existed to quench their hunger.

"When I say so, run back up the steps."

"We can take them. There's only four."

"No." Jack gripped the handle of his gun, freeing it from its holster. "Four is all we see, doesn't mean four is all there is."

"Jack, we can take them," she whispered.

Jack glanced at the four glitches that had revealed themselves. Ripped clothes, skin yellowed like jaundice, and glowing silver eyes, all turned on them.

"Run," Jack growled.

"We can take them. You have to trust me."

"Run!" He screamed, aiming his gun at the front glitch that launched.

Instead of following his orders, Emily leapt over the side of the escalator, her gun blaring. She took out the glitch on the right. Jack swiftly took out the remaining two.

"This way!" Emily shouted, heading to the front entrance.

"Emily, why didn't you run like I told you?"

"Are you serious, right now?" She paused; her gun still pointed in case of threats.

"You agreed that if we came out to this town, away from the safety of the base, that you would follow my lead."

"And I have been! I've been following your lead way before the breakout. Always doing as you command!"

"Apparently not. If you did, we would have left before we lost the sun. But no, you had to have the fucking snow globe! This way!" Jack took off the opposite way from the front entrance toward the back alley. He didn't wait to see if Emily would follow, but his shoulders relaxed a fraction when he heard her boots stomping loudly on broken glass.

The air crackled with tension as Jack led them toward the back of the storeroom. A crumpled exit sign dangled on the wall, its neon light blinked out forever. He pushed the exit door and it wouldn't budge. Throwing his shoulder into it, he pushed again, but nothing.

"It's locked," Emily said, dryly. "I had already swept this area and knew the backdoor was jammed shut."

"And you're just now telling me?" Jack narrowed his eyes.

"You wanted to lead so bad."

"You could have fucking told me!"

"Jack Johnson. Don't you dare curse at me."

He mumbled, his words slightly muffled by his mask.

"What? You have something to say, say it?" Emily folded her arms.

Even when she was upset and covered in protective gear, he still found her annoyingly cute. Instead of feeding into her fury, he turned his anger toward the jammed door. He slammed his shoulder into it again and the door budged. Something was propped against it.

"We should go out the front. The front is clear. We can see a wider range vs going out of the back. It's tighter, with less places to run and less places to hide."

Jack slammed up against the door for the fourth time, causing it to move a bit more. "We. need. to. go. To..." each word was full stomp as he threw himself against the door. "the. back. We. need. to. lay. low. Not. be. exposed." The door flew open creating a large CLACK as something metal ripped away and was thrown onto the ground. "See, it just needed the right touch."

Emily rolled her eyes. "You first," she said pointing toward the alley.

Before Jack could step over the threshold, snarls followed by a high clacking went off. Jack's eyes grew rounded.

Phasers shouldn't exist, they were annihilated. Yet, one stood before him, its hollowed eyes peering down at him. The phaser's mouth dropped open. Its jaw, unhinged and elongated, stretched to reveal rows of razor-sharp, serrated teeth, gleaming with an unnatural sheen. From its mouths, the toxic silver substance dripped. The clacking began at the back of its throat followed by hissing that sounded like a snake.

"Move!" Emily said, trying to slam the door closed. Before she could, a phaser hovered over Jack, its body wrapped in a hue of shadow like a mummy buried in a sarcophagus.

Jack raised his Cruiser and pulled the trigger right into its mouth while yanking Emily back into the store through the aisles. The clacking grew louder behind them as they found themselves returning to the lobby. More glitches greeted them. Their bodies moved in short broken snaps as they stumbled.

Through the glass windows, the setting sun cast a dark orange glow. At night was where these creatures grew in strength. Jack knew he needed to escape and fast. A memory flashed in his mind of his best friend being ripped to pieces in front of him. No matter what, he had to protect Emily.

Emily's gun went off before Jack had time to register a plan. His wife was popping the glitches in one shot and he joined her. Fighting side by side, they took the creatures down.

Emily screamed over the sound of snarls and flying bullets. "If you had listened to me, we would be in our van on I-west by now!"

Jack fired a shot right through a glitch's head, the bullet exited the back of it and into another glitch standing right behind it, a two for one.

"Are you really blaming me, at this moment?"

Emily placed her back against his. "I am. You never listen to me," she said over the growing moans of the glitches.

Jack reloaded, while knocking out a glitch with the butt of his gun. "We are here, aren't we! In this stupid ass Christmas store..." BANG, BANG, BANG. A spray of bullets took out five glitches. "...I don't get why you're so obsessed with this stupid holiday!" He shouted, his voice filled with bitterness. "Christmas was never my thing, and I certainly don't believe in some baby Jesus." Reload.

A gun went off right by his ear. Emily's eyes flashed with anger, her weapon firing relentlessly as she blew away a glitch on Jack's left. She momentarily paused, her gaze piercing into Jack's soul.

"Fine!" she retorted, her voice laced with defiance. "If you don't want to celebrate, then why are we here?"

"Exactly!" Jack yelled back. "I've been asking myself this the entire time."

"No, Jack." Emily said, her gun pointing from herself to him. "Why are we here? Why are we still doing this? Clearly you don't want to be together. An end-of-the-world doomsday didn't change that." Her words hung heavy in the air.

"Don't..." Jack ran a gloved finger through his dark hair. "...don't put this all on me!"

They screamed at each other. Their voices overlapped. This argument was bound to happen, why not now. Jack raised his gun and pointed it at Emily.

"That's right!" She bounced on her toes. "Won't you end me here. At least now you can get away with it, right!"

Jack pulled the trigger.

Emily's eyes grew wide behind her rounded goggles. Smoke rose from the barrel of Jack's gun as the last glitch fell to its knees behind her with a thud.

Through gritted teeth, Jack shouted, "Watch your fucking left!"

Emily's goggles fogged. She temporarily removed them, flashing a clear glimpse of her big brown eyes. She strapped the goggles back on, and asked, "Why are we still together? In this shitty marriage in this shitty world?"

Jack returned his 9mm to his belt and walked off.

"Maybe we shouldn't be."

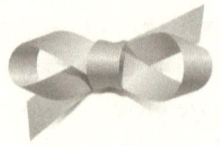

Act II

Night had fallen, casting a shroud of darkness over the store. Jack pushed a shopping cart to the side as he secured the front doors.

He loved his wife, but in times like these, it was hard to remember why. What happened to the shy woman that he met in college? She was different now, no, that's not right...she had been different way before the outbreak.

Jack wrapped tubing around the handles and gave them a hard pull. He then put a metal rod behind the sliding doors to make sure they wouldn't automatically open.

Jack allowed his thoughts to take him back before the outbreak.

He had gotten home early that day. He made his way up to the bedroom and opened the door. It smelled like fresh linen with a hint of jasmine from the flowers resting on the window ledge. The window was opened, a small gust of wind blew the white curtains. He could hear faint notes of his wife standing below on the back porch. When he got closer, her voice became clearer.

"I can't tell him, not now." She paced, curling a finger through her loose curly hair. With the other hand, she smashed the phone to her ear. Jack leaned in closer, straining to hear.

"I know, I know. But maybe he'll change. He has finally agreed to go to couples therapy."

Emily walked further into the backyard. She rubbed a finger across a sunflower, the yellow petals matched her sheer yellow dress, making her deep mahogany skin glow.

"Of course, I haven't given him the divorce papers. He doesn't even know I filed. I was waiting until after couples' therapy. Maybe...just maybe..."

A high yell came through the phone. Emily flinched, pulling the phone away from her ear. After the voice died down, she returned the phone back.

"Listen, I'm just not ready, okay! I don't want to start over again. I want him to communicate. I want us to light the fire again. We haven't had sex in six months!"

Jack's breath hitched. He was about to turn away until Emily's voice became hushed.

"What about him? It's over between us. We only met a few times, that's it. I haven't been with him recently, even when he comes to the house to visit Jack."

Jack's heart began pumping far too fast. The blood rushed to his head and the gardens below blurred.

"Listen, I'll call you back, sis. I have bread in the oven."

Jack swallowed hard, backing up from the window. The back of his knees met the end of the bed. He didn't remember when he had taken a seat. His mind raced, trying to process what he heard.

It couldn't be right. Wouldn't be right. She would never cheat on me.

Jack was deep in thought until he heard the subtle cracks of the stairwell as feet climbed to the top.

"Jack!" Emily said, clinging to her chest. "When did you get in?"

In a split second, he had to decide what he was supposed to do. He reached down, untying his shoe. "Just now." He forced a smile on his face. "That color..." He could see the nipple print budging through. "...it looks good on you."

"Oh," She stepped further into the room. "Thank you."

Pulling off his shoes, he rose from the bed. He crossed the room and pulled his wife in arms. He planted kisses on her forehead. His mind couldn't help but wonder who else had a chance to hold her.

He kissed both cheeks.

Did he kiss her like this?

He lifted her chin and studied her full lush lips.

Six months. He hadn't realized it had been that long not feeling the heat in between her legs.

Did he cum inside you?

"Jack." Her voice had become sultry.

He scooped her off the floor and laid her into bed. Pinning her arms above her head, he expertly ripped off his jeans and rolled up her dress. Her lips parted as a nipple slipped out of her sheer yellow dress. She widened her legs.

He wanted to insert himself roughly, instead he gripped her wrist and squeezed.

She let out a moan, the smell of her juices was intoxicating.

Fuck it.

He pushed in, the sweet caress of her warm walls embracing his erection felt like a deep tissue massage. Intruding thoughts attempted to pull him away from the grind of her hips.

Did you call out his name?

He thrusted deeper.

Did you call out his name!

He pounded into her.

"Jack!" Her body called to him and he answered.

"Say my name!" He let go of her wrist only to dig a fist full of her ebony ringlets into his palm.

"Jack!"

He pulled her head back to reveal her long brown neck.

"Yes, Jack. Please punish me. Please," she begged, her knees touching her breast.

"My pleasure, you dirty little slut." Jack bit into her neck. Her walls tightened, a gush of juices squirted onto his pelvis and dripped down his thighs.

Can he make you cum like me? He thought as he exploded inside of her.

There was a loud slam from behind him, snapping Jack out of his memories. He blinked rapidly; his hand instinctively went for his gun.

"Emily?"

Eerie silence.

Where had she gone?

"Emily!"

Shots fired from the back of the store. Jack took off down the aisles, jumping over broken shelves and trash. The back door was wide open.

A bloodcurdling scream pierced the air, ripping through the night like a dagger. Jack's heart leaped into his throat, his instincts kicking into overdrive. Another shot fired. He ran through the alleyway.

"Jack!" Emily screamed, her voice was cut off in the process.

Three men flung open black van doors and threw Emily inside. Jack fired, aiming at the vans ties. The van sped away screeching as it jumped the curb turning left.

Jack hauled ass after it. His mind was set on only a single target. He cut through a dark alley without a second thought, whipping past rotten corpses that smelled like raw meat prepped with spoiled eggs. He exited the alley, jumping in front of the van, holding out his gun.

He shot, the bullet made contact with the window on the driver's side, but it didn't crack. He shot repeatedly as the van picked up speed, racing toward him. Jack emptied the clipped, he reached for the reload. He could smell the oil from the van's engine. The clip jammed, he needed to shoot the tires. He reloaded, but it was too late. The van was on him. But he couldn't seem to move his legs.

The collar of his protective suit yanked, as he was thrown backwards onto the sidewalk. The van flew past without breaking once.

Jack didn't have time to register the snarls growing loudly behind him. He climbed to his feet, letting the bullets chase after the van that had now disappeared, heading north.

"Aye man, you need to save those bullets, there's a herd coming." A voice said behind him.

Jack didn't care. His wife was taken from him. He cursed himself.

I shouldn't have left her alone. I shouldn't let her go off by herself. If only we had left before sundown, this wouldn't have happened!

"Amigo!" Another tenor voice called. "We kind of need your help here."

Jack turned around, finally surveying his surroundings. Two men dressed in loose fitting clothes, outdated breathing masks, and old goggles, shot at ten glitches filling up the street.

Jack checked his clip, twelve in the chamber. Rage filled his every thought.

When I get a hold of the fuckers who took my wife, their lives will be forfeit.

He raised his gun and fired. Taking out all ten silver-eyed glitches with three rounds still left in the chamber.

He turned that smoking gun to the two strange men.

"Who the fuck are you?" He aimed at the smaller one's head.

"Whoa, whoa there, man. We aren't your enemies." The bigger one said.

"I don't know who the fuck you are, but you better start talking."

The smaller one with faded orange goggles, slowly put his weapon on the ground, urging the bigger man to do the same. They eased back up to a standing position, hands raised.

"I'm El." The small one pointed to himself. "And this is Pedro." El threw a thumb behind him to point at the larger man. "We were passing through when we heard screams. We thought we could help."

"So, you're not with those guys?" Jack flicked his gun.

"The rogues? God no." Pedro huffed. "I'd rather become a glitch then get caught with them."

Jack didn't lower his gun. He had never heard of the term rogue before. His eyes bounced from one man to the next.

"You don't know, huh man?" Pedro glanced at El.

Jack tightened his grip.

El stepped forward. "We're not trying to hurt you. And judging by your fancy protective suit and standard issued..." El gestured to Jack's face and gun. ".... everything, that you're not from around here. So, you don't know where the rogues have gone."

"But we do," Pedro said.

"Where?" Jack calmly brushed a finger on the trigger.

"They set up camp by the old Winterland," Pedro said.

Jack clenched his jaw, his trigger finger ready to pull. Instead, he holstered it and began walking down the blood-soaked street.

El called, "You're not possibly going there by yourself, are you?"

Jack heard the scrap of guns being picked up off the street. They didn't seem like the type to shoot, but his hand stayed on the hilt just in case. Boots picked up behind him.

"Amigo, that camp has super soldiers and you don't appear to be a super, but the way you just took out ten glitches, you might just be a soldier." Pedro said his breathing was heavy as he walked.

"I'm neither." Jack bent over and scooped up his wife's backpack from the side of the street.

"I think the best thing you can do is to stay out of that camp," El said.

"And let them take my wife!" Jack barked, his voice laced with desperation.

The couple exchanged a knowing glance, their eyes filled with empathy.

"Look man, I know how you feel. If someone took El, I would do 'bout anything to get 'em back." Pedro said gently. "How about this, we'll take you to the camp. Give you all the info we know. But we can't guarantee that we'll fight with ya." Pedro glanced at El. "Don't want to put him at risk."

Jack hesitated, his gaze shifted between the two.

"Then get to talking," Jack flung the extra pack over his shoulder and continued walking.

. . ◦‰◦ . .

About the time they made it to Winterland, snow had begun falling and coating the ground with a blanket of white.

"How long have you been married?" Pedro handed him a set of binoculars.

"Three years." Jack glanced through the lens. The park was lit up with colorful Christmas lights, broken fair rides, and old decorations that laid haphazardly amongst the rubble.

"I still consider three the honeymoon phase. I bet you two can't keep your hands off each other." Pedro sighed.

Jack shifted and the snow crunched underneath his belly as he laid flat to the earth. He didn't know why he said it, maybe to finally get it out in the open, but before he knew it, it admitted the truth.

"The marriage was over before it even got started." He continued looking through the binoculars, counting the guards lined on the walls.

"Why's that?"

Jack gulped. "I was never marriage material," he paused, not sure how much to divulge. "We met in college. She was this fresh eyed, ray of sunshine that made everyone glow and I..." He lowered the binoculars. "...wasn't even supposed to be on campus. I was doing a job and getting rid of the evidence when I bumped into her. The moment she flashed her smile at me, I knew I had to have her."

There are ten guards in total.

"We need to get closer," Jack said.

Pedro and Jack used the cover of the night to wind their way to the side gate.

"So, what did you do?" Pedro dropped down on his belly. "To get her?"

"I lied." That was the simple truth. He watched her for weeks then molded himself to fit her every need. When he had won her, he thought he could really change. To actually be the man she truly deserved, be perfect. Just like that stupid ass snow globe. He was selfish, he knew. But a part of him wanted to be normal. And if he couldn't have it with her then he knew he couldn't have it at all.

"Did she ever find out the truth?" Pedro reached for the binoculars. Taking his turn and scanning the new area.

"No." He had been careful. Too careful, completely shutting down the side that made him a monster. Until he began taking jobs again and having to hide the blood stain clothing, the late nights, and the weekends away from home. Just being near her he feared that she would see him for what he really was. He withdrew almost immediately after the vows were confirmed.

"I think you should tell her." Pedro lowered the binoculars.

Jack shook his head, while checking for extra clips. He dug in his pack, he should have prepared more, but he was out. He pulled out his wife's pack and checked to see what she had inside.

"She wouldn't understand. She wouldn't love me as I am."

"You wouldn't know that unless you communicate with her. You might just be surprised."

Jack pulled out the snow globe. The perfect scene of the house, the carriage, and the kids, set frozen inside. A life he had been attempting to give her.

Pedro continued. "When I first met El, I didn't think he would love me or even find me attractive. I'm a beast and he's..." Pedro chuckled. "...everything I wasn't. I'm a lot like you in the sense that I tried too hard. Molded myself to fit his world, damn near starved myself. Spent three months in the hospital, developed what doctors called an eating disorder." Pedro made himself comfortable. "I just wanted him to look at me."

Jack lifted his eyes to Pedro, tightening the snow globe.

"You know, you can only pretend for so long before the truth eventually reveals itself. Luckily for me, when I finally got up the right amount of courage to confess my love to him. He accepted me, fully as I was. I was shocked. I guess a part of me thought nobody ever could. That I had to be something else. Someone else. You know?" Pedro looked thoughtfully at the starless sky.

"And if he didn't..."Jack watched the fake snow fall inside the globe. "...accept you? Then what?"

"You move on. Rejection hurts, yes. But forcing a square to fit in a triangle hurts worse. All that time wasted."

Jack transferred the snow globe into his pack. He wanted Emily, needed to have her, be near her, and if the choice was to lose her or force himself into her perfect snow globe of a world then he would grit his teeth and do so, even if it hurt. Luckily, he liked pain and torture.

He continued searching her pack until his fingers brushed across metal. He pulled out three knives, and three rounds. That's thirty-six clips.

He quickly reloaded. The crunch of snow under a heavy boot was heard to his right.

"It's El." Pedro pointed to a bracelet on his wrist. "We're synced. Just in case we lose track of each other."

Jack nodded, making a mental note to purchase one for him and his wife.

El joined, giving them an update.

"The gods must be smiling down on you tonight, mi amigo. There are only two super soldiers on the east. They are outdated models, still strong as fuck, but one bullet to the head would kill them for sure. Let me show you where they're holding your wife."

They followed El to the west side of Winterland. Jack scanned the scene.

"Amigo." El pointed to an area where there were cages filled with people and children.

"Hey, man." Pedro whispered. "Your wife is wearing a similar issued protective suit like yours, right?"

"Yeah."

Pedro handed Jack the binoculars then pointed him to where he needed to look.

Below, Jack spotted Emily. He could tell it was her by the way her suit clung tightly to her figure. She was outside the cages moving like a cat in the night. She snuck up behind a guard who was taking a piss and slit his throat where he stood. The man was dead before the last of his piss even hit the ground. Emily dragged the guard's body to the side, then patted him down. She yanked keys out of the dead man's pocket then rushed to the kid filled cages and unlocked them. Then she went to the next cage, until everyone had been released.

"Are you sure your wife needs rescuing?" El said.

Jack had just asked himself the same question. He had always seen her as someone to protect. The only innocent thing he had left in this mad world. The only beacon of light.

Who was this woman? Jack watched as Emily guided the crew of captives to a cut out section of the gate. When the last woman and child made it safely through. Jack was on his toes waiting for Emily to exit as well. She didn't. She turned back, snaking her way through the cages and heading deeper into the park.

"What the fuck is she doing?" Jack grinded his teeth.

"I don't know, but she has trouble to her right."

Jack swung his binoculars to the right. Two super soldiers, with their bionic arms, were headed right towards her.

"You better get down there, and fast. We'll provide cover." Pedro pulled out his long shooter. "Aye man." Pedro tugged at Jack's arm. "Tell her before it's too late."

Jack slung his pack over his shoulders and glanced from El to Pedro and nodded; without another word, he shot down the slopes.

Entering in the same way the captives were set free, Jack maneuvered across the dead soldier with a cut throat and his dick out, frozen. He followed the path Emily went down, hoping he would make it in time.

Act III

The snow fell relentlessly, blanketing the decrepit fairgrounds in a shroud of icy white. Jack trudged through the frozen wasteland, his footsteps leaving faint imprints in the snow. His mask, ear protectors, goggles, and suit kept out most of the cold. Soft music played, he knew that tune. Christmas Fairy. He followed the music that was soon drowned out by a scream.

Jack picked up pace. Up ahead, he saw Emily backing away, her hands up. Her goggles cracked, her mask falling apart. The super soldiers stalked her with twisted smiles on their lips. Pedro was right, judging by their make and model, these S. S's were outdated. Which confirms they can die with a bullet to the head, just like a glitch.

"Whoa guys." Emily stopped, hands held high. "I'm just a woman. Harmless, innocent, woman. I got lost. No need to gang up on me." She stopped.

"Oh, really?" The bigger S.S. touched his swollen cheek. "That punch you gave me said otherwise."

The second S.S. laughed.

"If you're so harmless. I'm sure you would much rather spend it with me instead of in the cages. You know, to make up for this little misunderstanding."

Jack wanted to pull the trigger right then and there.

He must die first.

Using this as an opportunity to sneak up behind them, Jack crossed over then ducked underneath a rusted slide. He had to be calculated and precise, one mistake and an S.S. could end his life. His heart pounded, echoing in his ears, adrenaline surged through his veins,

115

reminding him of his primal desire. Protect his wife and live. He was at the perfect angle now.

He lined his gun to the sides of the S.S.'s temples.

Steady. He repeated to himself. Snow quickly covered his outstretched arms. The S.S.'s heads were in unison. He pulled the trigger, the bullet cut through the crisp air leaving mist in its wake. One soldier had scooted forward at the last minute while the other was shot directly in his skull. His body immediately slumped forward, face first in the snow. The remaining S.S. turned to face him, its eyes filled with malice.

Jack repositioned his gun and shot again. The S.S. dodged, running directly toward him. Jack jumped from behind the slide, each bullet hitting every spot except the kill spot.

Stop fucking moving! Jack clenched his teeth. The S.S. was about to strike when Jack's gun clicked empty. Jack reached for this knife, but the S.S. was too fast. Instead, he braced for an impact that never came.

· · ⚜ · ·

A gun went off. Scarlett droplets exploded from the middle of the soldier's head and onto the white snow. The S.S. looked shocked as if his brain hadn't yet caught up to what had just happened. He spun around to face his killer and there was Emily, smoke rising from the barrel of her gun. The soldier dropped to his knees then face planted into the snow.

Blood pumped to Jack's other head as he met his wife's murderous gaze. He ran to her, pulling down his mask and ripping off her torn one. He had to kiss her and if he was honest with himself, he needed to fuck her, right here in the snow.

When their lips separated, he could taste the honey on her tongue.

"You came for me!" Emily said in between kisses.

"Did they fucking hurt you?" Jack checked for any signs of distress.

"No, I'm fine. I swear."

"Let's get out of here." Jack attempted to drag her to the gates.

"I can't. Not yet." She snatched away from his grasp. "There's this little girl who they took. I need to save her."

Jack proceeded to argue but Emily's set jaw told him that she had already made up her mind. She was going whether he would come or not. Jack walked to one of the dead S. S's. and kicked his limp body onto his back. He bent down and stripped the soldier of his mask, wiping some of the blood off with the man's clothes.

"You need to protect your mouth," he said, handing the mask to her.

Emily nodded, grabbing the mask and wiping the inside out with her fingers. She clicked it on. "This way."

Jack pulled his mask back on and followed her from tent to tent before finally stopping at one.

"She's in here!" Emily rushed inside. Jack surveyed the area, they needed to move fast.

He was sure those gunshots would have brought them attention. He ducked into the tent, allowing the flaps to fall behind him. Inside, there was a single cot with a pillow and blanket with overturned beer cans at the foot. To the right, Emily began picking at a lock that withheld a girl inside, she looked no bigger than ten. Her teeth were razor sharp like a shark, her dark hair was piled on top of her head, and her pale skin was browned by layers of dirt.

The cage lock clicked open. "We need to move."

Jack went to the cot and ripped the sheets until he created a mask and a little coat to cover the girl. Emily took what he had and helped the girl into it. She pushed the child's hair back.

"Are you okay?"

The child nodded.

"We will have to move fast once we leave the tent. Stay with me, okay." She comforted the kid.

The child turned weary eyes to Jack. Emily followed her gaze then turned the girl's eyes back to her. "That's my husband. He's good, okay? We won't hurt you." Emily rose to her feet, bringing the child over. "Jack, this is Miling. Miling this is Jack."

Jack took his hand off the hilt of his gun and shook the girl's hand. "Nice to meet you, Miling. Stick beside us, no matter what, and we might get out of here safe."

"Jack." Emily shoved him.

"I'm telling her the truth."

An alarm sounded.

Times up.

Jack followed Emily through Winterland, his Mossberg 500 Cruiser pointed as they ran. Miling clung to Emily's side. The snow falling had added a few extra inches to the ground. The air reeked of rotten flesh mixed with spoiled eggs. That could only mean one thing, glitches.

They rounded the corner headed toward the cut in the gate when several soldiers stopped them in their tracks. Shots fired echo in the distance, followed by yelling of commands.

"Drop it," A soldier said, pointing an M15 at Jack.

"You first." Jack pointed back.

The soldier laughed. "Do you really think you can defeat all of us?"

Jack assessed the situation. One S.S. and the other six looked like regular soldiers, but he couldn't be sure until he saw them move. He could only assume that they would think the same about him.

Emily raised her gun in one hand while Miling growled like a puppy whose voice has yet to drop.

"Awe, that's cute." The soldier holding the M15 said. "I suggest you drop your weapons, and we can wrap this night up. Okay?"

There was a click coming from Emily's gun. She looked over to Jack. Her eyes read, "Do you trust me?"

He nodded. For the first time in a long time, he realized that she had become more than the young innocent girl he met on a college campus.

"Enough of this." The soldier said. Right before he spoke again, a voice came over the walkie talkie on his shoulder.

"We need backup! Send all units!"

The surrounding soldiers kept their stance.

"Kill them." The main soldier commanded.

Before one could get a bullet loose from their chamber, one of the six soldier's heads exploded as they dropped to the ground. A second one then a third hit the snow and bled out. The remaining soldiers broke their formation as they looked around them, trying to figure out where the shots were being fired.

Jack saw this as an opportunity to pull Emily and Miling behind a metal ride and out of harm's way.

"What was that?" Emily said, ducking as shots continued to fire.

"I met some friends." Jack reloaded his gun.

"You and friends? That's new." Emily said. A bullet whipped passed overhead.

Miling snarled, chomping her teeth as if she was biting the air.

What a wild thing. As soon as Jack thought this, Miling took off from behind the metal covering. Emily tried to pull the girl back, but Jack held her in place. More shots rang out, closer this time, the scent of rotten eggs picking up on the wind.

The glitches were nearby.

Emily struggled to go after the girl, "Let go!" She shouted, but Jack refused. Instead, he pinned her down while risking a look over the metal ride.

Twelve feet away, a soldier was lifted off of the ground. His face exposed, his lips pressed hard together trying to hold in a frantic scream. The yellowed nails of the phaser stabbed into the man's chest as if the phaser was wrapping its claws around the soldier's spinal cord.

The man screamed, and in the scream, death was upon him. A long red tongue dove into the soldier's mouth. His eyes, nostrils, and ears began leaking silver like uncoagulated blood. The soldier went limp as the phaser withdrew its tongue.

Jack dropped back behind the metal ride. *If only we can get outside the gate, we can distance ourselves from the chaos.*

"Phasers are here. We need to put as much distance between ourselves and this place, now." Jack turned to Emily.

"I'm not leaving Miling."

"You can't save everyone, dammit!"

"I'm not leaving without her." Emily said through clenched teeth.

"So, you will risk your own life to save someone who you barely know? What about me?"

"What about you?" Emily pushed her hair out of her face.

Jack sat back on his heels trying to block out the screaming coming from a few yards away.

"If we make it out of here alive, I think it's time for us to finally go our separate ways." Emily said, softly.

"We can't do this here, not here." That's all Jack could manage to get out. After all this time, he couldn't let her go.

"Then when, if not now, Jack?" Emily swallowed hard.

Jack rubbed the barrel of his gun to his temple, not wanting to hear her next words.

Emily reached out and touched his hand. "Man-eating glitches, creepy ass phasers, super soldiers kidnapping me. All of that I can handle, but sleeping every night with a man who refuses to talk to me, touch me, or even look at me!" There was a crack in her voice. "I thought I saw another man in you when we first met, but that man has been long gone," she said, getting to her knees, prepping to walk away.

Tell her the truth. Pedro's voice played in his ear. It was hard for even him to accept, so how in the hell was the love of his life going to accept it? He had been forcing her into the darkness, away from the monster, too scared to touch her, corrupt her. He was ashamed of who he truly was, how could she love him despite it? He was worse than the crooked S. S's, the glitches, and the phasers combined.

"David," Jack said, the name of his dead friend left a nasty taste in his mouth.

Emily paused; the snow fell upon her raven hair. Such beauty in this disaster.

"I knew about the affair and the divorce papers."

A body being ripped into two while a soldier screamed echoed through the park. Jack's skin prickled; the hairs of his neck stood. If they weren't going to make it out of this, he might as well tell her the truth. "The night of the first glitch attack, I went over to his house to confront him." Jack shook his head. "I went over to kill him," he corrected, watching Emily who stared back with wide eyes through snow covered goggles.

"I had it all planned out. You see, killing him and getting rid of him would have been nothing for me because that is what I did before I met you. A professional hit man. When I bumped into you on campus, I was there completing a job. When I saw you, for the first time in my life, I thought that maybe there was something else I could live for." Jack took his 9mm and held the barrel to his temple, scratching the side of his head. "I don't know what the fuck I was thinking. I thought if I changed..." he stumbled for the words. "...give you the perfect snow globe of a life. The picket fence, the house, the perfect cars, the perfect children then I could finally leave all this shit behind and retire in your arms. But it wasn't enough."

A snarl came close to the metal ride. Blood pumped through Jack's entire body giving him the strength to quickly reach over the ride just as a glitch bent down to meet him. He pulled the glitch over to their side, held his gun to the glitches forehead and pulled the trigger. Silver blood exploded onto his goggles. Jack grinned, allowing all of who he tried to hide for all these years to fall away like rotted flesh.

"A glitch ripped out David's throat right in front of me and you know what I thought?" His eyes narrowed at Emily. "How dare you take my prey!?"

Jack remembered it like it was yesterday. The sun peeked in a cloudless sky, birds chirping in a sleepy suburban neighborhood. David, the little fucker he befriended in order to pull off his normal guy life facade, was pulling his trash cans to the end of the street. A toothy grin plastered his face. Jack remembered the heat of his palm over the coolness of his gun handle behind his back. Then the glitch ran from across the street and ripped David's throat out before Jack could intervene. Jack raged, emptying his clip into the glitch without even thinking what or who the thing was.

"You married a monster." Jack wiped the silver from his goggles with a gloved leather hand. "And if you leave me, I will hunt you down to the end of earth and kill anybody who dares to lift a finger your way." Jack reached into his pack and pulled out the snow globe. "I can't give you this life. The life you deserve—" Before Jack could finish his sentence, Emily yanked down her mask and then his and kissed him, long, deep, and hard. Her teeth bit across his lips sending little pinches of pain to his hardened dick.

"Emily," he grunted, shocked by her sudden outburst.

Her lips ripped away as a glitch rushed from over Jack's shoulder. Emily yanked out her gun, shooting the glitch clean in the forehead. Without a second to waste, another glitch headed from behind Emily.

"Behind you," Jack said, his nine at the ready. Emily turned like a black hurricane and pulled the trigger. Perfect shot as the glitch's head blew back causing its entire body to lift from the ground, spin, then crash into the snow. Emily turned back to Jack, a wide grin lit her face. Jack rose to his feet, a bit unsteady, unsure. "I'm a monster," he said, trying to convince her to abandon him.

She licked the barrel of her gun then blew the lingering smoke. "And I'm a monster fucker."

All the wind was knocked from Jack's chest. His heart had never skipped a beat, but in this moment, it had skipped several.

Emily bent to pick up the snow globe. "All I ever wanted, you idiot, was for you to tell me the truth. You think I'm that stupid that I didn't know who or what you were?" She glanced at the snow globe. "I never wanted this. I wanted us, you're my perfect happily ever after." She shook the globe, white swirls of fake snow flared inside. "Even if that means exchanging this world for yours." She dropped the globe onto the ground. "I'm not as innocent as you make me out to be," Emily grabbed Jack's hardness which was pressed against the zipper of his pants.

Jack took his hand, reached behind her head, and grabbed a fist full of her hair, pulling taunt.

Emily continued. "Nor do I want to be. This is who I am Jack, who I've always been. From the moment I met you, I saw the killer in you, the same one that's been in me."

Shouts rang out, snarls, ripping of flesh, screams of sheer panic, Emily's hand gripped on his dick, the playful smile on her lips, made his head swim.

"I'm a killer too, Jack. And in this fucked up dystopian world, we can finally be free."

"You're mine," he growled.

Emily's grip tightened. "As much as I would love to take you here, right now. We need to move."

They kissed again and for the first time, the world was right. Repositioning their mask back onto their faces, Jack followed Emily's lead as she took down an S.S. and a glitch.

Jack's heart swelled with pride. How did he not see it before? Her fierceness, her strength?

Distracted, a phaser rose in front of him, and wrapped its claws around his chest. Jack aimed his gun and let out as many shots into the mangled shadow's hollowed eyes. The phaser exploded with a howl that sounded more animal than human. It's silver blood soaking the snow. Jack dropped back to his feet and quickly reloaded.

Back-to-back, he caught up to Emily as they were surrounded by a beautiful cacophony of guns blasting, which lit up the night like fireworks. When Jack ran out of bullets, Emily threw a double barrel shotgun his way.

"Miling!" Emily yelled. Jack turned just in time to see Miling jump on top of an S.S. Her razor-sharp teeth bit into his neck. Miling tore away from the S.S. with a mouth full of his flesh. Before the soldier could hit the ground, the little terrible monster jumped off his shoulders and onto a glitch running past. Another bite, followed by wild clawing, made the glitch go limp where it stood. The gunshots died down and the screaming had stopped.

Miling rode the glitch to the ground then rose to her bare feet in the snow. Her smile was crimson mixed with silver. Emily began walking to her. Jack reached out to pull her back, but Emily nodded, dropping to one knee, and throwing her arms open. Miling skipped over to her and tucked herself close to her chest.

"Good girl," Emily said. "You're coming with us."

Jack cocked his head. "She's not affected?"

"Nope." Emily pushed the girl's hair back. "She's a variant, a human not affected by the change of the glitches. Apparently, headquarters were hunting them down and locking them away for experiments." Emily turned to Jack. "Can we keep her?"

A moan came from Jack's left. An S.S. was crawling slowly in the snow. Jack took his shotgun and blasted the soldier in the back of his head. Afterwards, he bent down to one knee.

"Is this truly what you want?" He studied Emily's eyes through her goggles.

"This is all I ever wanted."

The guns had stopped firing, the snarls and grunts had gone silent. Snow continued to fall over old rusted roller coasters and broken

Christmas lights as the tune of Christmas Fairy hummed in the background.

This, Jack thought. *This was the perfect snow globe.*

Jack reached out his hand and pulled the women in close. "We will need a new home." He smiled down at Miling, "One with plenty of toys, bloody-silvered eyed toys."

E.A. NOBLE

"Have the audacity to have faith in yourself. When no one else is willing to defend you, have the courage to stand. When silenced, have the determination to speak up. Write what no one else can with the conviction that you have within. Finally, rest. This is something your ancestors could only hope for. Allow them to rest in you." — E. A. Noble

E.A. Noble was raised in Jackson, Mississippi, and was encouraged to dream by her grandmothers. They compelled her to read, write, and keep a journal. Poetry was E.A.'s first love since it gave her the freedom to express herself in a way that no other activity could.

Since then, E.A.'s pen has changed into her keyboard, and her journals into worlds without end. She is now listening to the advice of her ancestors as she dares—for the first time in her life—to share her talents with the world.

Her Fantasy novel, When Fire Meets Earth, is available online.

You can reach E.A. Noble at her website, https://www.theeajournal.me/[1] .

---

1.   https://l.facebook.com/

l.php?u=https%3A%2F%2Fwww.theeajournal.me%2F%3Ffbclid%3DIwAR1ZaapG5pDx6rdC

HjtNHSCNNomT8qp2sZnRTp6eW14Ao71EUYq3XdeDaZ8&h=AT1LZfGhJgEUWKjknEo

djw6zC9OQQ3vqOVrwuCFhMbc_aiucxwdVh-Q9LYpIUC3t-Ri3dJPXyOX8T2l1Az27Sv9KYrblOFJ9yMwRjP1CI8y--Ik5R4P0u8z_9h9PXBnjq1Qh-nlVovKkszRoqZfk-Q

Christmas with the Carters

by Mo Flames

Unwrap the gift of family drama this Christmas - it's the gift that keeps on giving!

Get ready to deck the halls and stir up some drama this holiday season with Desiree and Derrik Carter. Their first Christmas with both families together was supposed to be a merry gathering, but when one of Derrik's sisters decides to give tradition the cold shoulder, the family dynamic takes a frosty turn. As if that wasn't enough, unexpected guests arrive and the family gets snowed in together, making it impossible to escape the drama. Can the Carters keep their cool and mend the fractures in their relationships? Will they end up singing carols or slinging insults come Christmas day?

Follow Desiree and Derrik as they navigate the highs and lows of family, love, and the true meaning of the holiday season.

CHAPTER 1

Desiree Carter's stomach lurched as she folded another sweater into her suitcase. She covered her mouth and swallowed hard.

"This is it for their outfits and I'm going to finish getting my stuff packed." Derrik said, while holding up a set of identical red sweaters. "Hey, you okay, baby girl?"

"Umm yeah, I'm fine," she said, quickly removing her hand. "I was just thinking if I was forgetting anything."

Derrik nodded before he returned to packing. Desiree was thankful he turned away as another wave of nausea washed over her. She steadied herself against the bedpost, waiting for it to pass, hoping he wouldn't look up and see her struggling. Out of the corner of her eye she watched as Derrik zipped up their sons' suitcase while humming along to Donny Hathaway's, This Christmas. He then moved on to organizing his toiletry bag in another suitcase. This would be their second Christmas together as a family since their sons were born, but the first they would be spending it with both of their families. He looked so excited. She couldn't wait to see his face when she told him her secret. Not yet. She wanted the moment to be perfect. Desiree slipped a palm over her still-flat belly, imagining the new life inside. This year's holiday would be their best one yet.

Happy that the queasiness was gone, she returned to her task of packing her suitcase for their trip. Shortly after he finished packing, Derrik came around and embraced her in a loving hug, swaying to Love You More At Christmas Time. He might've been the CEO of a music label, but her husband couldn't sing a lick. Desiree giggled. "Please let Kelly do this on her own."

"Damn, and here I thought I was doing something serenading my wife."

"You tried it, but no. Stick to what you're the best at and that's discovering the talent."

"I know something else I'm the best at."

Desiree let out a surprised breath when he held her butt, leaned in, and his lips softly brushed against hers. A passionate kiss ensued, leaving her breathless and in a state of pleasure. She could taste him on her lips and murmured with delight. "Mmhmm."

He withdrew from the kiss slowly, caressing her cheek lovingly. "Yeah, and as much as I want to finish this, I'll have to as soon as I get back. I promised Patty and 'nem I was going to come through. I might shoot some hoops with them. After that I need to make a quick run to the store. Jayde said she's not coming unless I bring Uno Flip or Uno All Wild."

Desiree laughed, "You better get them cards then."

"I swear she gets on my damn nerves," Derrik grumbled. "Need anything while I'm out?"

Her heart quickened. This was her chance. "No babe, I'm all set," she gave him a quick kiss.

When he left the room, she went over to their bedroom window. She waited for his Bentayga to pull out of the driveway and watched until it was nothing more than a speck in the distance. Desiree rushed into their master bathroom, kneeled in front of the cabinet, and pulled out the pregnancy test she'd been hiding. Nerves and excitement battled in her stomach as she followed the instructions. She set the test on the counter, hands shaking. In under three minutes, she'd know for sure. Desiree perched on the edge of the tub, leg bouncing. She placed a hand on her stomach. A baby. Their baby. Dylan and Dykota would be big brothers.

Three minutes crawled by. Desiree closed her eyes, picturing Christmas morning. Derrik's face lighting up when he opened the box wrapped in a tiny bow. The joyful tears in his eyes. The timer beeped. Desiree reached for the test. Two solid lines stared back at her. Pregnant. This was really happening.

She pressed both hands to her mouth, laughing and crying. A few minutes later she emerged from the bathroom. After taking a picture with her phone, she carefully hid the test in a different box, and packed it away in her belongings. Then she went over to the bed and sat down. Desiree dialed her best friend, Brielle.

"Hey diva!"

"Hey diva!"

Desiree heard the voices of her twin sons parroting in the background. She stifled a laugh shaking her head while Brielle chastised them.

"No boys. Remember, I'm the only one that can call her that. It's Mommy, not diva or Desi, do you understand?"

"Yes, TiTi." They said in unison.

Desiree chuckled. "Girl, I told you those two will repeat everything you say."

"Tell me about it. What's up? We have a few more stores to hit up and then we'll be on our way."

"Remember I was telling you how I've been feeling sick and—"

"Desi, are you pregnant?" Brielle hush whispered.

"I am! I took a test right before I called you."

"Yaaay! I hope we get our princess! How excited is Derrik?"

"He doesn't know because I haven't told him. I want to wait for Christmas to let that be his other gift, but I don't know if I can hold out a week."

"I don't know if I could. You know that man has been trying for another baby, too. These boys be running my pockets, but I don't care. I hope we get a set of girls."

Right then, a wave of nausea hit Desiree. She covered her mouth and swallowed, but she felt the bile coming. "Bri, gotta go. Feeling sick. See you when you get here."

Desiree ended the call, ran to the bathroom, and emptied her stomach of everything she'd eaten earlier that morning. Once she got through the last bout of dry heaving, she flushed, and went to the sink to brush her teeth. Her boys were an easy pregnancy with minimal nausea and no vomiting.

Looking in the mirror at her figure, she rubbed her flat belly. "I guess if you're going to be Derrik's princess, you're going to give mommy hell, eh?"

She went downstairs and relaxed on the sectional sofa in their spacious family room with high vaulted ceilings. After they were married, Derrik sold his house and purchased an eight-bedroom, seven bath, mansion for their family in the new subdivision, Crest Hills. Their twenty-thousand square foot home sat on a hilltop location, spanning eight acres, with gated access. Everything she and Derrik wanted was included in the custom-built home's contemporary features, which expertly struck a balance between elegance and a warm, cozy feel. Desiree powered on her laptop and started surfing the web for baby items. She'd been sitting there for more than a couple of hours before she heard his voice.

"Baby girl, you in here?"

"Yeah, babe I'm in here." Desiree quickly closed out of the browser and glanced up from her laptop.

Derrik entered the family room and made his way over to the sofa where she sat. When he stood in front of her, her gaze traveled from the Air Jordans up his athletic legs to the basketball shorts where her eyes briefly landed on the swell of his dick. He gripped his package and cleared his throat. She moved her eyes up to his chiseled chest and bulging biceps underneath the sweaty tank top. Her cheeks reddened when their eyes collided. She imitated him, tucking her bottom lip in her mouth.

He let go of his lower lip and moistened both of his before winking. "See something you want?"

"I sure do!"

Desiree hurriedly placed the laptop aside and rose from the sofa. She was mere inches from him. Sweat and his musky, masculine smell filled her nose. She ran her fingers over his chest and leaned in as Derrik bent his head. He slid a hand behind her neck guiding her to his face. His mouth slanted over hers. As she partially opened her mouth, his tongue slithered between her lips.

She could taste the saltiness of his sweat mixed with the minty fresh flavor on his tongue. Desiree felt the hardness of his dick pressing against her thigh. She rubbed her hands over his smooth head, gyrating her hips and dry humping on his stiff shaft. The moment his lips touched hers, a wave of pleasure flooded her body, and she had to stifle a moan. He made a low sound of pleasure into her mouth, moving his hands to her ample backside, massaging, and kneading it like dough.

"Really, you two?"

"Daddy!"

Derrik groaned before withdrawing from their kiss. Desiree grinned while he fidgeted with his shorts to push his erection down. He placed his forehead on hers and in a low growl promised, "Later, Mrs. Carter." He gave her a quick peck before turning to his sons who came running. Scooping them up in his arms, Derrik quickly supported their little bottoms and lifted them off the ground. Dylan and Dykota clung to him by wrapping their arms around his neck. He planted kisses on both of their cheeks.

Dylan scrunched up his face as his voice shrilled, "Daddy, you wet!"

"Well, Daddy's been playing ball so I'm a bit sweaty."

"You need a bath!" Dykota's face mimicked his brother's expression as he fanned in front of his nose.

Brielle walked up joining Derrik and Desiree in laughter. "Those two right there, stay throwing the shade."

Derrik bent down again, setting the boys on the floor. He tussled their curly tops. "All the time, Bri. Before they say anything else, let me go take a shower." He winked at Desiree. "I think they need a nap so we can finish what we started."

"Okay." She nodded, holding out her hands. The twins each grabbed one and stood next to her. "We'll be in the kitchen."

"Umm, that right there is exactly how y'all are gonna end up with another baby or babies. Keep it up." Brielle chimed in.

"I know. That's what I'm hoping for." Derrik gave Desiree a quick peck on the lips and made his way out of the family room.

"You think you're so slick egging him on. Let's go feed these two so we can put them down and practice." Desiree gestured with an upward head nod for Brielle to follow her.

"TMI, diva. I saw enough of the practice when I walked in."

When they reached the kitchen, Brielle helped Desiree get the boys in their highchairs. She set banana halves and applesauce cups in front of them. After she got their sippy cups of milk, she grabbed a couple of bottled waters, and sat down at the large island bar next to Brielle. She twisted off the cap from her bottle and took a swig before asking, "How were they today?"

Brielle finished gulping down her water before answering. "As always, TiTi's babies were good."

"We were good!" the twins parroted in unison.

Desiree whispered, "Okay so like I told you earlier, we gotta be extra careful when talking around them especially cussing. Dykota cussed at Mommy the other day."

The look on Brielle's face was one of embarrassment. She slapped her forehead. "Shi-uhh, yeah, he probably got it from me."

"Oh, we know he did. He didn't hear it on CocoMelon or Loo Loo Kids." She leaned in. "We're pretty sure he's never heard us say, 'Oh, bitch, please.'

Brielle's eyes grew big, but she laughed when Desiree smirked.

"Mommy asked if he said it. I had to play it off and tell her no, but it was loud and clear that's what he said."

After her fit of hysteria subsided, Brielle wiped the tears from her eyes. "I'm sorry, Desi but that just took me out. I know how his little voice sounded when he said it."

"It took everything for me and Derrik not to bust out laughing. That caught us off guard as it always does when they learn knew words or phrases."

Brielle turned her head to take a peek at the boys. Both smiled and with a mouth full of the bananas they shouted, "TiTi, we were good!"

"Yes, y'all were TiTi's big boys today. I'm so proud of you." She turned her head toward Desiree and whispered, "Yeah, they're going to put y'all asses through it. Forget Dennis, they're Dylan and Dykota the menaces."

Desiree nodded while taking another swig from the water bottle. "Girl, tell me something I don't know. Derrik doesn't help egging them on either."

An alert chimed from Brielle's phone. She grinned as she picked it up and started typing. Desiree knew more than likely she was texting Justin. Desiree leaned in, peeking over her shoulder. "So, Peaches, what's up with Justin? Is he coming with us?"

"Bitch, you kn—" She glanced back at the boys. They were busy eating their applesauce and obviously hadn't heard what she said. Brielle returned her attention to Desiree. "Heffa, you know not to call me that."

Desiree laughed, fully aware Brielle hated when they teased her about the endearment Justin gave her. He'd told Brielle not only was her ass shaped like a peach, but she tasted like it too. "Okay, Bri, is he?"

Brielle cut her eyes before she smiled big and declared, "Yes, girl. After I sent him a pic of that cabin mansion, he said he wouldn't miss it. Oh, I didn't tell you. Why has he planned a romantic getaway to St. Lucia for Valentine's Day."

"Oooh, St. Lucia is beautiful. Hmm, sounds like the perfect place for a proposal."

Brielle waved her hand. "Nope, I'm not setting myself up like that."

"What do you mean? Y'all haven't talked about marriage?"

"Of course, we have. But I don't want to do that to myself. You know, overthinking everything he's doing and guessing if it'll be on this holiday or the next. When he's ready, he'll ask."

"You're right." Desiree agreed before taking a moment to check on the boys. She noted their fluttering eyes as they sipped the milk. "Come on, help me get the boys cleaned up and down for their nap."

After getting the boys settled, Brielle and Desiree were heading into the family room at the same time as Derrik. He came from behind and kissed the back of Desiree's neck.

Brielle wagged a finger. "You can wait to do all of that when I leave."

"Well, you need to head on out before I ravish my wife right here in front of you. We don't have long before the hell-raisers are awake."

"Say less. I'm outta here."

"Let me walk you out." Desiree offered, heading behind her.

Brielle waved her off. "No, diva, you stay. I can let myself out. Just make sure to call me when y'all head out. See you in the mountains. Love y'all. Bye!"

Derrik barely waited for Brielle to leave the family room before he executed a smooth move, dropping low and picking Desiree up in his arms. She squealed but instinctively encircled his waist with her legs while slinking her arms around his neck. He peppered a few kisses on her cheeks and lips before moving into a deeper, more passionate kiss. As he trailed his lips down her neck, she let out a throaty moan.

"Babe, are you planning to ravish me right here?

"Mmhmm."

"Where Hodges or Nate can just walk in on us?"

Desiree's eyes widened when he looked up at her, his lips twisting into a teasing grin. Derrik leaned forward and whispered against her lips. "Maybe. Got a problem with that?"

A thrill shot straight to her core as his hand slid inside her pants.

"No." Desiree quickly shook her head.

"Good. Now let's get these off. I'm starving."

She lifted her hips to help Derrik slip her panties and yoga pants off. He placed his hands under her butt, cradling both cheeks, and buried his face in her hot, hungry center where it ached for pleasure. His tongue swirled back and forth around her bud. Desiree rubbed her hands across his smooth, clean-shaven head, and pushed him closer to her pleasure point. Derrik understood what it meant and clamped down on her quivering nerve cluster with fervor. The muscles in her stomach clenched and she slammed her eyes shut, in anticipation of the forthcoming series of climaxes he was sure to bring. Desiree's body shuddered with pleasure as he expertly licked and teased her sweet spot.

"Ooooh ... babe! Right there! Yes! Right there! Oh god! I'm-I'm coming!"

The pressure building inside evaporated in a rush of euphoric contentment. Desiree grabbed onto Derrik's shoulders for stability as she trembled through a series of deep breaths. Her cheeks were flushed from the incredible sensation that still pulsed throughout her body.

When Desiree finally opened her eyes, she found Derrik staring back at her with a big smile on his lips. Derrik leaned toward her, his intense gaze never leaving hers. He advanced along her body, lightly dancing over her skin with gentle kisses. Every inch of her skin was a map for him to explore, every curve an invitation to indulge. His tongue delicately touched the love bites he had left behind, causing her to tremble in pleasure underneath his touch. He moved his head up to kiss her neck, nibbling playfully before he pulled away. His hands moved lower, gently caressing the insides of Desiree's thighs with delicate finesse. She gasped in pleasure when Derrik's fingers delved between her warm slit and into her moist center. Desiree's back bowed with the sensation, feeling her inner walls widen around his agile digits as he plundered the depths of her with expert knowledge.

His lips brushed over her ear as he spoke in a low, seductive voice that sounded like gravel. "Baby girl, I can feel your pussy gripping my fingers. Are you about to come again?"

"Y-yes! Yesss!" Desiree screamed in a voice she'd never heard before. It felt as if her body had been set on fire. She took in deep breaths of air as the waves of an intense climax crashed through her body, sending tingles through every nerve ending. Her limbs trembled beneath the weight of the sensation, and her heart pounded in her chest.

It wasn't until her breathing began to slow that Derrik withdrew his fingers. He brought them to his lips, lapping up every trace of her essence from the knuckles to the tips, before rising to his feet. With an ease that seemed effortless, he removed his sweatpants and changed places with her, so that she was now seated on top of him. They maintained eye contact as he lifted her up and slowly guided himself inside. Desiree groaned in ecstasy as his girth filled her, pushing against the tender walls of her insides. He cupped her butt, supporting her as he started lifting and lowering her in rhythm with his movements. She clung to his shoulders for balance. They moved gracefully together. Their bodies worked in unison seeming like one combined entity rather than two separate ones as their pelvises met over and over again until both reached an incredible climax together.

"Derrrik!"

"Desi! I'm ... oh ffffuck!"

Desiree felt his body tense up and then the throbbing of his dick inside her. Within seconds, her orgasm followed suit with her insides contracting again. Their rapid breathing and pounding hearts were perfectly in unison. She gave one last quiver and they both exploded together. Derrik held her close until their breathing slowly returned to normal, his hands caressing her back while they basked in the afterglow of their lovemaking.

They sat quietly for a while before he finally spoke. "Baby girl, that was amazing as always."

"I know it really was." Desiree murmured softly nuzzling closer.

Derrik kissed the top of her head and squeezed her tighter. "I don't know what you've got planned to give me, but let Santa know I've been a good boy. I'm trying to get all this pussy for Christmas."

Desiree giggled. "Oh, don't worry babe, I promise you're getting this and even more."

CHAPTER 2

Derrik watched from the front door as the SUV rental pulled into the circular driveway. Hodges had driven to the airport to pick up his sister, Jayde, despite her protests on getting a rental. Since they weren't familiar with the city, he wasn't about to let her travel that far to their vacation home alone, especially after she told him that her twin, his youngest sister Jordyn, wasn't joining them for the holiday getaway. He still hadn't told their mom considering he didn't know the reason behind Jordyn's sudden change of heart. Jayde omitted that part, only explaining Jordyn wanted to stay with a friend. She stepped out of the SUV tossing her long, sandy brown tresses over her shoulders. As always, it was neatly styled, not a strand out of place. She wore a cashmere sweater in a rich emerald hue, perfectly coordinated with her wool trousers and riding boots.

"Hey, I'm glad you made it here safely." Derrik said when she reached the door. He pulled her into a tight embrace.

"Yeah, you made sure I would with Lurch over there."

"How many times have I told you to stop calling him that?"

"What makes it worse is that he groans like him too whenever I try to have a conversation or ask him something." She looked over her shoulder before glancing back at him. Jayde mimicked the television character with a grunt and began laughing hysterically.

Derrik playfully mushed her head. "Will you knock it the fuck off."

"I thought I heard you in here." Olivia said, walking up to them.

"Hey, Ma."

"Uhh, where's Jordyn?" She looked past her out the door.

143

Jayde's eyes found Derrik's before bouncing back to their mom's. "So, about that ... umm Ma—"

"What's wrong? Is she okay?" Olivia frowned, her eyes searching Jayde's.

"Yes, Ma of course, she's fine. But ... umm err, well she won't be joining us for Christmas this year."

Olivia inhaled sharply, her face falling. She blinked rapidly. With visible effort, she composed herself. "But, but I don't understand. Why? When I spoke to her yesterday, she-she didn't say anything about this. What made her change her mind? Did you two get into a fight?"

"No! And why would assume it's something I did, Ma?"

"I'm sorry. It's just, well this just comes as a surprise."

Jayde lifted her shoulder in a partial shrug. "Well Ma, you know she's dating Nico now and those two have been inseparable since they reconnected. From what she told me he wanted to take her to meet his parents."

"Who?" Derrik chimed in.

Neither Jayde nor his mom answered his question. Instead, his mom released a sigh of frustration. She rubbed her temple. "I don't get it. She talks to me about everything else but didn't bother telling me this. She knows I depend on her to help me with most of this stuff. Why wouldn't she say something if she knew she was going to be up under him?"

"Ma, this is exactly why. She knew you would likely make her feel guilty about wanting her to be here." Jayde shook her head.

Derrik could see his mom attempting to maintain her composure, but the hurt was evident in her eyes.

"But it's always been our tradition. Ever since you girls were little," her voice cracked slightly. Olivia shook her head, the frustration mounted in her tone. "I know you said they've reconnected, but how come his family gets to meet her and we haven't even met this guy? Hmph, and everybody will be here except her. She knows this was our time as a family. Why would she want to go be under his family? It just feels like she's abandoned us."

"I understand how you feel, Ma especially not knowing about this guy." Derrik directed a serious expression toward Jayde who responded with a nonchalant shrug. He shifted his gaze back to their mom, his tone soft and compassionate. "But getting upset won't change things. Let's focus on everyone that is here and try to make the best of it. We can still have a wonderful holiday together."

Jayde stepped closer, squeezing Olivia's hand. "Derrik's right, Ma. Let's make the most of this time together."

Olivia took a deep breath, nodding slowly. Her expression softened. "You're both right. We'll make this Christmas special, no matter who's here or not."

The three exchanged hugs. Hearing Luther Vandross crooning out Every Year, Every Christmas, the familiar sounds of the holiday continued around them. However, Derrik could feel with Jordyn's absence, this year would be different.

"There's Aunt Jay," Desiree said to the twins as they were making their way down the hall. The boys bolted from her and toward them.

"Aunt Jay!"

"Munchkins!" She knelt with her arms open wide.

Desiree glanced at Derrik with a frown, but he immediately shook his head in response, motioning for her to come near. He grabbed her hand and tugged her closer. His lips moved close to her ear as he softly spoke, "Jordyn's not coming. She's decided to spend it with some guy. Ma's not happy of course."

With a silent nod, Desiree stepped away from Derrik. She greeted his sister once their sons finished showering her with hugs and kisses.

"Oh, how I've missed these two. I need to come and visit more. They're getting so big. Every time I see them, it seems like they've grown at least an inch." Jayde ruffled their curly hair.

Dylan shouted, "Gammy O says we're growing like weeds!"

"We're bigger than weeds right, Gammy O?" Dykota questioned.

Everyone laughed, while Olivia knelt to his height and cupped his face. "Yes, Kota baby. You are so much bigger than weeds." Then she gave both boys a peck on the cheek.

"Hey! What's going on in here? Oh good, y'all finally made it."

It was his dad, Vance.

"You need some help, Pops?" Derrik asked, gesturing toward the tangled ball of lights in his hands.

"Yeah. Since your mom's got some help now with Jordyn ... wait, where is she?"

A heavy feeling descended as Derrik watched his mom's face drop. She got to her feet from kneeling with the boys and exhaled sharply. "According to Jayde, she's not coming. She decided to go be that boy she's been seeing and spend it with his family."

At first his dad frowned, but then he tipped his head in acknowledgement. "Well, no need in being upset about it, Liv. The girl is always under you. I told you one day she was gonna find somebody. Which meant she was gonna get out and date. She can't do that hanging off your titty all the time."

"What?" Olivia gasped. The initial surprise on her face switched. She shot a fiery retort in return. "She does not hang off my titty, Van!"

Dykota tugged on Derrik's pant leg. "Daddy what's a titty?"

"Titty!" Dylan clapped and echoed.

Desiree shot Derrik a horrified glance while Jayde cackled with amusement. Derrik hurried to do damage control with the boys while his parents continued their banter.

"Oh, yes, she does. If she were here, she'd be standing right here attached to it."

"Please Van, you know they're both always with me."

"Not Jayde so much. She's not hardly under you the way Jordy is, and you know it," Vance refuted.

"But Jordyn knew I needed her to help me. She knows how to cook."

"Hey, I know how to cook too!" Jayde threw her hands up to object. "If you wanted me to help, you could've asked me, Ma."

"She sure could've, but see she only does stuff like this with your sister. That's because she's the baby. I told you, always on her titty."

"Titty!" Dylan and Dykota shouted at the same time.

Derrik let out a deep sigh of frustration. "Pops, come on. I'm trying to get them to forget the word."

Olivia immediately wagged her finger, chiding Vance, "Didn't I tell you Derrik said the boys repeat everything they hear. Now look at what you've got our grandbabies saying."

Vance lifted his shoulders. "But you said it too. And ain't nothing wrong with the word. Y'all acting like I done cussed. Didn't you breastfeed them, Desiree?"

"Yes sir, but I umm—"

Olivia interrupted her to continue fussing at Vance. "That's not the point, Van. I'm quite sure they haven't referred to her breasts as that."

"Exactly, Pops. It sounds tacky for them to be saying it." Derrik chimed in while rising to his feet. He'd just finished talking to the boys. He'd been honest and done his best to explain why the word in question wasn't appropriate for them to use. Not that it mattered. At some point Derrik knew his sons would blurt out their newfound knowledge—and the word that went along with it.

Desiree scooped up Dylan. "You know what. I think it's time for your naps anyway."

"But I don't wanna take a nap, Mommy." Dylan pouted and pushed his lips out.

Derrik was all seriousness as he spoke firmly to him. "Dyl, it's time for a nap."

Dylan shyly looked away from him and buried his head against Desiree's shoulder. Derrik gave Dykota a stern look, who went over to his aunt, shrinking away.

Jayde lifted him effortlessly into her arms. He burrowed himself into her embrace. Then Jayde offered her assistance to Desiree. "Since I've got Kota, I'll help you put them down."

Derrik gave Desiree a kiss on the forehead before moving over to Dylan and giving him a peck on the cheek. "See you later okay, buddy." Then before Jayde could walk away, he gave Dykota the same.

"They're such sweet little boys. They remind me a lot of you, Derrik times two." Olivia sighed contently.

He chuckled, "We're trying, Ma. I'm sure you know, as sweet as they are, they're a handful."

She nodded.

His dad interrupted their moment. "Okay, son, you offered to help. We better go and get that tree looking festive. I don't wanna get fussed at anymore." He held up the tangled lights.

Olivia grumbled. "Yeah, you better. You're skating on thin ice, Mr. Carter."

"Better than being in hot water, my sweet Liv. Now gimme some of that titty, I mean some sugar." Vance wrapped his arms around Olivia as she tried to resist him. She let out a giggle before surrendering to his lips, which he pressed against hers in a tender, sweet kiss. Derrik observed his parents, amused at how they still flirted with one another like when he was a kid.

When Vance released her, he gave Olivia a playful smack to the backside when she started to sashay away. "Mmhmm, see son, that right there is what I'm talking about. No enhancements. Yo mama is that natural, sexy brickhouse the Commodores were singing about." He bit into his bottom lip and shuddered. "I'll never get tired of watching her walk away."

"Okay, yeah, I'm good. Don't need to hear anymore. I'm going so we can get to work on this tree. You don't want to get fuss at, right?" Derrik didn't wait for his dad to respond as he pivoted in the opposite direction and headed for the family room.

When Vance joined him, he handed Derrik the knotted ball of lights. Together, they carefully took their time to untangle them. After about fifteen minutes of work, they finally loosened all the knots and were ready to adorn the nine-foot-tall Fraser Fir tree with the assortment of colorful bulbs. They worked in companionable silence for a while before Derrik noticed his dad's troubled expression.

"You okay, Pops?"

Vance sighed. "Just thinking about your sister. I think I might've struck a nerve saying that to Liv. Even though Jordy's always been the one under your mom, I've noticed she hasn't been around much. Your mom has been looking forward to hosting this with your in-laws coming and well ..." He trailed off.

Derrik had been thinking about Jordyn's sudden absence from the family and being unaware of her recent behaviors with her new boyfriend. When he'd attempted to get more information, both his mom and Jayde brushed him off saying the guy was no harm. It would take some getting used to her not wanting to be around them for her relationship considering she was always under their mom. He nodded in acknowledgement. "I know. But it's her choice, right? One thing y'all have taught us to do is picking the path that we want to. We've gotta respect that."

"You're right," Vance conceded. He playfully chucked Derrik under the chin. "When'd you get so wise, son?"

Derrik rolled his eyes good-naturedly.

Just then, they heard a commotion coming from the front of the house. Hodges walked in and before he could announce him ...

"Ho ho ho! Black Santa Claus is here to bring some merry cheer!" boomed Uncle Vic, Vance's twin brother. He stepped into the family room, his arms piled high with packages of various sizes and colors.

Derrik smiled to himself. He knew his uncle would do just that: bring merry cheer and provide much needed comedic relief.

CHAPTER 3

Desiree ended the call and squealed. "My mom and dad just pulled up. I'll go let them in. Babe, can you let your mom and dad know they're here? And Jayde do you mind getting them cleaned up please? Or y'all can switch."

"No, of course, I've got 'em. Derrik, before you do that, can you get help me get them down?" Jayde playfully pinched both of their noses before removing their empty plates from the food trays. "Gammy O made y'all some delicious pancakes and now you're all sticky."

"But I'm not sticky!" Dylan held up syrup-covered hands.

Dykota mimicked his brother, raising his hands. "See, I'm not sticky too!"

"Oh yes, you both are. And now Aunt Jay has to wash your face and hands. You don't want to get this sweet stuff on your Paw Paw and GiGi, now do you?" Derrik asked while unbuckling the straps of Dylan's highchair. He then carefully lowered him onto the floor.

Dylan whined, "But GiGi says I'm sweet, Daddy. Please, don't let Aunt Jay wash off my sweet."

"I couldn't wash it off if I wanted to. You'll always be sweet, Dyl." Jayde reassured as she guided them out of the kitchen."

"Me too, Aunt Jay?" Dykota asked.

"Yes, you're my sweet Kota! Now come on. Let's go wash our hands."

Desiree shook her head as she headed for the front door. Her boys were a riot and brought so much joy. Instantly thinking of how their family of four would be increasing soon, the corners of her mouth curved upwards. Five days. That was how long Desiree had until she

151

could tell Derrik and the rest of their family about her pregnancy. She couldn't wait. Excitedly, Desiree pulled the door open feeling a chill breeze from the mountain blowing against her face.

Once they stepped into the large foyer area, Desiree closed the door behind them and without hesitation she ran to her parents, wrapping them in a loving hug. "Mommy! Daddy!"

"Pumpkin," David said, his gruff voice muffled in Desiree's shoulder as he squeezed her tight.

Juanita joined the hug, and the familiar floral scent of her perfume punched Desiree's senses. Immediately a wave of nausea attacked her. She quickly withdrew from their arms and covered her mouth.

"Oh! Err, I'm sorry. But excuse me. I-I need a minute."

"Desiree, sweetheart, are you o—"

She didn't give her mother a chance to finish. Desiree bolted from the foyer, down the hall to the bathroom. Thankful that Jayde had taken the boys to the bathroom on the other side of the main level, she made it there in time to expel her breakfast, and what seemed like her dinner. Desperate to muffle the sound of her retching, she turned on the faucet and flushed the toilet. Luckily, by the fourth bout of heaving, her boys' boisterous voices, and excited welcomes from the rest of the family provided enough noise to mask her gagging noises. A few minutes passed and she finally felt better. Thankful they had a staff that stocked all bathrooms with toiletries, she took some of the mouthwash and rinsed her mouth. Desiree took a few seconds to compose herself before grabbing the handle of the bathroom door. She slowly opened it, stepped out, and right into her mother's inquisitive stare.

"Mommy?" Desiree swallowed and quickly pointed behind her. "Did you need to use the bathroom?"

Her mother took a step closer and squinted her eyes. "No. I came to check on you. How are you feeling, Shelly?"

She knew it would be pointless attempting to keep anything from Juanita Thompson. As a district attorney, she had an uncanny knack for detecting deceit. Desiree glanced down the hall where their family were gathered, chatting cheerfully amongst themselves. Directing her gaze back to her mother's eyes, she sighed under her breath. In a hushed voice, Desiree spoke. "I'm feeling better. I was dealing with a bit of morning sickness."

"Oh, Shelly!" Juanita beamed, cupping Desiree's face.

She slipped out of her mother's grasp and craned her neck to peek down the hallway again. Thankfully, no one heard her mother's outburst of joy. Desiree shifted her gaze back to her mother. "Shhh! No one knows except Bri and well, now you. I know you're going to tell Daddy. Please, Mommy nobody else. Not even your bestie Liv. I wanted to surprise Derrik for Christmas."

Her mother pulled her into another embrace and whispered, "Your secret's safe with me, Shelly." Then she released her, grabbing her hands. "Look at you, already glowing."

"I don't know about glowing. I'm pretty sure I have his princess growing in here. She's already being a brat not letting me keep anything down. I know I look green."

"No, not at all. You're just as beautiful as ever. Oh, I'm so happy for you!"

Desiree squeezed her hands. "Thank you, Mommy. It's so good to have you here. Come on, let's get back before they come looking for us."

As they made their way down the hallway, everyone had moved into the family room. Her dad, Jayde, and Derrik's parents were socializing and having a good time. The luxurious vacation home they'd rented for the holidays was impressive, with oceanic oak floors, high ceilings, and windows stretching from the floor to the ceiling. It made Desiree wonder if she should talk to Derrik about buying a property like this one—somewhere they could return with both of their families year after year. As if her dad had heard her thoughts, he asked Derrik the same thing.

"Derrik this place is enormous. Juanita showed me the pics but being in here now. Wow, how did you find it? I'm at a loss for words to describe it. To be honest, I'm surprised you don't already have one for yourselves."

Before he could respond, Desiree interjected. "I know, Daddy. I was just thinking to ask my husband if we can get one like it. I think we need to make this an annual gathering with our families."

"GiGi!"

The boys bolted over to Desiree's mother. Juanita went to her knees. As soon as they reached her, they threw their arms around her in a tight hug and nearly knocked her to the ground.

"Whoa, boys! Y'all are about to knock GiGi down." Desiree moved over to help with getting Dykota while Juanita steadied herself.

Dylan exclaimed, "GiGi, I missed you!"

"I missed you too!" Dykota echoed.

"Can I get some sugar?"

Desiree felt an immense swell of joy in her heart when Dylan planted a kiss on her mom's right cheek, and Dykota kissed the left.

"And I missed you too my sweet grandboos." Juanita then enveloped both boys in her arms. She released them and rose to her feet to greet Vance and Olivia. "It's wonderful to be together again. I'm looking forward to this weekend with all of you, especially my girl, Liv."

Olivia came over and snaked an arm around Juanita's waist. The two women embraced each other tight. "And I'm so happy you are here. This is going to be one of the best holidays yet." Olivia declared.

Just then the doorbell rang.

"I'll go get that." Derrik stated as he made his way out of the living room.

Vance turned to Desiree. "Janelle's not expected to be here until tomorrow. Were y'all expecting anyone else?"

She nodded. "Yes. More than likely it's Bri and Justin. They should've been here before my parents, but Bri wanted to check out The Village in downtown. She said there's some shops she wanted to poke her head in, so they stopped there first."

A few seconds later, Desiree realized she was right—it was indeed her best friend's voice she heard coming from the front of the house.

"No, we've gotta take them to this amusement park, then to see the lights and of course, Santa Claus. And there's this cute lil shop where they make the candles right there. There's so much food, Derrik. They have games, live music, and somebody told us there's even a parade going on. I think it'll be really nice."

Brielle walked into the room with Justin following. She greeted everyone with a big smile and waved. "Hello family!"

"TiTi!"

The boys went running over to her and Justin. He helped with picking them up so Brielle could shower them with affectionate kisses. They placed the boys back on their feet and, along with Justin, moved around the room to greet Desiree and Derrik's parents.

Brielle held onto Olivia as she spoke. "It's so good to see everybody again. You all look good. I'm trusting that everybody's doing well."

Everyone nodded. Derrik clapped his hands. "Hey look, y'all are just getting here. We need to show y'all where your suites are in this big place before we get our evening of fun and festivities going. Desi, I'm sure you've got your parents. I can handle taking care of Bri and Justin."

"And we'll handle keeping these two occupied until y'all come back." Jayde offered.

"Okay sounds like a plan." Desiree said and then she gestured to her parents. "Let me show you to your room."

Her parents followed her to the second level to one side of the floor where the master suite was located. She understood their oohing and ahhing over the floor plan. She'd never seen anything like it either. This enormous 10,000 square foot vacation cabin didn't skimp on luxury. It had high-end contemporary finishes throughout its nine master suites, a nursery, ten and a half bathrooms, a theater room, a massive game room, and an indoor heated pool with spectacular views. Unlike other cramped cabins designed to fit as many people as possible, this one was all about extravagant comfort.

"Here's your room," Desiree said, opening the door to reveal a spacious room with a four-poster bed. She guided her parents further into the bedroom to show them around. They had one of the nine master suites, featuring a king pillowtop bed, and their own ensuite bathroom with walk-in tiled showers and corner Jacuzzi tubs. The two large windows let in abundant sunlight, offering direct access to the backyard deck. "Make yourselves at home!"

"Seriously, Pumpkin the pictures did this place no justice," her dad complimented while setting their luggage next to the bed. He wandered over to the window. "It's even better in person. I wouldn't be the least bit shocked if Derrik didn't already purchase this for you. He's always surprising you with doing something over the top."

Her dad unlocked the door leading to their balcony and then pulled it open. He stepped out onto the platform, to take in the view of the mountains.

Desiree winked at her mom and flashed a mischievous grin as she hush whispered, "Well, Derrik's not the only who can have big surprises."

CHAPTER 4

"Derrik!"

When Derrik opened the front door, his older cousin Janelle, made her way into the house, launching herself at him. He laughed, struggling to keep his balance against her enthusiastic, tight embrace.

"Girl, let me go!"

"Nope, I haven't seen you in months. You gon' get all this loving. Now bring your big 'ol Charlie Brown head over here. Muuuuah!" Janelle gave him a wet kiss on the cheek and let out a boisterous laugh.

"Disgusting!" He playfully pushed her away and wiped his face with the back of his hand. "I have no idea where your mouth's been." Derrik's laughter died on his lips when he glanced past Janelle and spotted none other than Khloe Dillon, his former lover, standing just a few feet away. He'd never expected to see her, and of all places, here. His face contorted into a frown.

Janelle was oblivious to his reaction, chattering excitedly about how happy she was to see everyone after so long. She pulled back to look Derrik over critically. "I know my daddy made it here. Where's everybody else?"

Ignoring her question, Derrik scoffed. "Why is she here?" His gaze flicked to Khloe again before returning to his cousin. "What were you thinking bringing her here?"

"Will you relax, cuz. She ain't here to cause problems. Trust me, she don't want your ass no more. Right Klo?" Janelle turned around to face her. "Tell my cousin why you ain't hardly pressed for him. No matter of fact, why don't you show him."

"Babe, your mom asked who was at the—"

158

He whipped his head around to see Desiree coming down the hallway. Her hazel eyes were like a pair of high-powered binoculars, zooming in on Khloe. Before he could even get a word in, she'd already launched into her tirade.

"Nah uh! Oh, hell no! This ain't about to go down. What is she doing here?"

Janelle threw her hands up. "Hold on, Desiree please. I was just trying to tell Derrik that Khloe was gonna show him why she ain't studying him no more." She nodded toward Khloe to give her the floor. Go 'head, now you can show both of them."

Khloe looked from Desiree to Derrik and raised her left hand. Janelle pointed to her ring finger. "That's why. Your girl is engaged if y'all hadn't heard."

Derrik's eyes swung to Desiree. She was staring at Khloe indifferently. Her expression betraying nothing. Personally, he didn't care about Khloe's relationship status, and he knew his wife felt the same. Khloe represented one half of the partnership that was behind an elaborate scheme to break him and Desiree apart, as well as embezzle money from Desiree's employer a couple of years ago. Derrik needed answers as to why his cousin had brought Khloe there in the first place.

Desiree's narrowed gaze left Khloe and cut to him. She shook her head before snorting. "No, we hadn't heard. Nor do we care." His wife twisted her head to his cousin, asking the same questions he'd been waiting on the answers to. "Janelle, what is she doing here? Why on earth would you bring her knowing the shit we went through behind her psycho friend's fuckery?"

"See, I told you this wasn't a good idea, Elle." Khloe finally spoke up in a soft tone.

Desiree responded with a heavy layer of sarcasm, shooting an icy glare at her. "It sure as hell wasn't."

"Elle?" Derrik frowned at his cousin. He'd never heard anyone call her that. "Since when you started going by that name?"

Janelle ignored him, turning to address Khloe instead. "No, this was a perfectly good idea."

"How do you figure?" Desiree retorted. "You know full well she and that lunatic were living in the land of de-lu-lu. How could you easily forget they could've cost me and my unborn babies' lives? Your cousins, Janelle."

Khloe opened her mouth to reply but Janelle beat her to it, whirling around to face Desiree.

"She had no control over that!" Janelle yelled.

In response, Desiree bellowed. "Might as well have! She was in cahoots with his crazy ass plans for everything else!"

"You know what, Elle, I didn't come to cause any problems. I thought you talked to them about me being here. I should go." Khloe took a step back and turned to walk away.

Desiree folded her arms across her chest. "Yeah, you should."

"No! You don't have to go anywhere." Janelle exclaimed as she cast a glance at Derrik while outstretching a hand for Khloe to stay put. "Auntie O said I could bring a guest, and Khloe is my guest."

Derrik rolled his eyes and shouted in frustration. "Now you know damn well my mom didn't mean her!"

"Hey! Hey! What's going on out here?"

It was his mom who'd joined them in the foyer.

"Hey, Auntie O! Hmm, come here. I've missed you!"

Derrik looked on with disbelief as Janelle practically threw herself at his mom in an overly dramatic display of affection. She was doing the most for nothing. His mom wasn't going to let the woman who had caused so much upheaval in their household, stay with them for the holidays.

Olivia eased out of her arms, laughing. "Janelle, girl, let me go with your silly self. Now why did I hear your loudmouth all the way in the kitchen? What are you and Derrik arguing about now?"

Janelle's uneasy gaze found his and Derrik cocked his head, arms firmly planted across his chest. His tone was dripping with sarcasm as he posed the question to her. "Yeah, Elle what were we arguing about now?"

"Elle?" His mom's expression was one of confusion.

Derrik gave a slight shrug. "Uh huh, I'm not sure who came up with that name either, Ma."

Janelle clicked her tongue against the roof of her mouth and glanced between the two of them several times. She deflated slightly, letting out a resigned sigh. "Auntie O, did you say it was okay for me to bring some friends?"

"Yes. I told you it would be fine." Olivia nodded her head in agreement.

Janelle gestured toward Khloe as she spoke. "Okay so, I asked Khloe, her fiancé, and his friend to come—they'll be here tomorrow. But anyway, so umm, the reason ... sadly, Khloe's mom passed away a couple of months ago. Her dad has been gone for years. She's an only child just like me. I know what it's like to be without your mom the first year. Even though she has Bakari, she's my friend and I-I wanted to be there for her. I'm not trying to cause no drama. But I thought, well ..." Janelle paused for a beat while Derrik cast a piercing glance at her before she continued. "Khloe's still my girl. I already told them she ain't have nothing to do with what that psycho did to Desiree. And—"

Derrik didn't want to hear it. He waved a hand. "Nah! You don't get to brush it aside like that shit didn't happen, Janelle."

"I'm not, but y'all coming at her like she had something to do with what that man did to y'all. She couldn't control what he was gonna do."

Derrik's face contorted in anger as he barked, "That's beside the point, Janelle! You didn't think about asking how we would feel before springing this on us!"

Janelle's eyes grew wide. "You act like I set out to do this on purpose!" she raised her hands in defense.

"Why didn't you call? You call any other time especially if it's about money or some other nonsense."

"Money? Some other nonsense. You can't be serious right now!"

"Okay, enough you two!" Olivia yelled, standing between the cousins as a buffer. "All I wanted was for my family to be together and we couldn't even get this right. Y'all always end up in some kind of disagreement. Why can't we just get together without this bickering. Yes, you should've let them know she was coming, Janelle. This is quite unsettling considering the history everyone has."

• • ⚘ • •

"I know Auntie O, I guess I wasn't thinking it would be an issue with this amount of time passing. Looking at it this way, I can see how it was selfish and inconsiderate of me. I'm sorry. I was just looking out for Klo like I said. She's without her mom and I get that. I mean, what can we do? She's here now."

Olivia nodded and turned to Khloe. "Honey, I am so sorry for your loss. Janelle's right. You shouldn't be alone. You're more than welcome to spend Christmas here with us. There's more than enough room."

"Thank you, Ma—uh, I mean, Mrs. Carter." Khloe's voice came out quiet, her eyes filling up with tears.

Desiree blew out an audible breath of frustration. Derrik grabbed hold of her hand and gave it a comforting squeeze. He was appalled at the fact that his mom had given in to Janelle's tactics. Despite hearing of Khloe's mother passing away, he was unsympathetic and unmoved. Derrik disagreed with his mom allowing her to spend the holidays with their family. He opened his mouth, but his mom threw up a hand.

"Derrik, your family is safe and sound. They have been for the last year and a half, right?"

His eyes locked onto his wife's. It was clear she wasn't thrilled about it either, but what could he say or do? The threat against her was no longer there. She was safe, his sons were safe, and they'd moved on from that whole ordeal. He couldn't go against his mom, but he could try to make his concerns known. Derrik acknowledged her with a nod. "Yeah, Ma but—"

"No, Derrik there are no buts." Olivia looked around at each of them and spoke in a pleading tone. "Look, I don't care who is here so long as we are here, loving on one another. Can't we just focus on that?"

Derrik's mouth was set in a tight line of disapproval. "Whatever," he muttered under his breath. Without even glancing at Khloe, Derrik shot Janelle a dirty look and then proceeded to guide Desiree down the hallway. His thoughts were running wild, trying to predict how the rest of the week would unfold.

One thing was for certain, it was going to be a holiday unlike any other.

CHAPTER 5

Desiree sat on the edge of the bed, peering out the window at the snow-covered trees. She felt Derrik's warm body against hers when he wrapped his arms around her and placed a kiss on her neck. "You good, baby girl?" he asked, nibbling at her ear lobe.

Desiree turned to face him. "Yeah, I'm just thinking about how everything's going to be now that Khloe's here. This wasn't exactly how I pictured our holiday with the family to go."

"Hey, neither did I. Sure, I hate that happened to her but don't let her fuck up our vacation because of it." Derrik pulled her closer.

She nuzzled her face into his neck. "Okay I won't."

"She can't fuck up what we got, baby girl. I'm yours and nobody else's."

Desiree smiled, feeling the warmth of his tight embrace. "I know, and you're mine too."

She tilted her head. Her heart raced as she deepened the kiss, savoring the sweet taste of Derrik's lips.

"God, I love you," Derrik said, pulling away to look into her eyes.

Desiree felt a rush of emotions, knowing how lucky she was to have such a loving and devoted husband. "Come here," she whispered, beckoning him with a crooked finger. She went in for another kiss, their bodies pressing against each other in passion.

"You're so gorgeous," he murmured into her ear, his breath warm on her skin.

"Thank you," Desiree replied, feeling her cheeks heat up. She tilted her head up to meet his gaze. "But not as handsome as you."

"Flattery will get you everywhere," Derrik teased, pressing a gentle kiss to her forehead. He held her close for a moment, his fingers tracing gentle patterns on the small of her back. "I want you to know you are the only woman I have eyes for, Desiree Carter."

Her heart swelled with love for this man who'd captured her soul. "And you're the only man I'll ever need, Derrik Carter," she said, reaching up to loop her arms around his neck.

Derrik's eyes searching hers for confirmation. "Promise?"

"Promise," Desiree breathed, sealing their commitment with a tender kiss.

The air around them seemed to crackle with intensity as Desiree moved closer, her fingers caressing at the nape of his neck. Their lips met again, this time with a fiery passion that left no room for doubt about their love for one another. Derrik's hands roamed over Desiree's body, each touch igniting a wave of desire within her. Desiree felt herself pulled helplessly into the whirlwind of their lust, her body responding eagerly to his touch. She marveled at the way his fingers knew exactly where to caress, how his mouth could make her forget everything but the exquisite sensation of their connection. She reciprocated, her hands exploring the taut muscles of his back and shoulders. As they moved together, their breaths mingled, becoming faster and more ragged with each passing moment.

"God, Desiree," Derrik grunted, his voice rough with need as he trailed hot, open-mouthed kisses down her throat. "You drive me insane." He squeezed her breasts together, alternating between licking and sucking both nipples to rigid points.

Her nails raked down his back, as she arched up into him, urging him closer. "Derrik ... I need you," she rasped, her voice barely audible over the pounding of her heart.

He raised his head with a mischievous smile and shifted his body to hover above her.

"Desi," Derrik breathed while their foreheads remained close together, his eyes never leaving hers. "I love you so much."

Desiree's heart swelled at his words. She knew he meant it with every fiber of his being. "I love you too, babe," she whispered back, pulling him in for another kiss, savoring the intensity of his love and devotion to her alone.

Derrik retreated from her mouth long enough to slide between her legs, settling himself at the juncture of her thighs. His thick mushroom head pressed at her damp entrance. Impatient, Desiree reached between them, but Derrik knocked her hand away. He smirked and plunged into her. She whimpered and writhed under him as he filled her. Her inner walls rippled, closing around his shaft, hugging him in an ultimate embrace.

"Fuck, baby girl!" Derrik groaned, pausing for a moment. He rocked his head vigorously back and forth.

Desiree could tell from the strained expression on his face that he was struggling to hold back. She locked her legs around him, holding him captive to her lust. Her body sucked him in, holding him tight. He bucked his hips, rhythmically plunging in and out of her. Each thrust sent her reeling into bliss. Their bodies moved together in perfect harmony. A raw, primal energy thrummed between them that seemed to defy logic, a connection that went beyond the physical and drew them deeper into the realm of pure emotion. Their lovemaking reached a fever pitch that neither had ever experienced before.

"Oh-my-God, Derrik ... it feels. I'm ... I'm coming!"

Derrik grunted, "Shit! Me too, baby girl. Arrrgh!"

As the waves of pleasure subsided and they were both left gasping for air, Derrik held onto her tightly. "Wow," he murmured, pressing kisses to Desiree's damp forehead. "That was ... damn, baby girl I don't even have words for it."

"Neither do I," she agreed, her heart still pounding in her chest.

Derrik brushed a strand of hair from her face. "If I didn't know better, with my swimmers I'd say you just got pregnant."

If only you knew. Desiree laughed softly, the joy in her eyes radiating as she gazed up at him. "Well, we'll just have to wait and see, won't we?"

Their moment of peaceful contentment was shattered by the loud, piercing ring of Desiree's phone. With a sigh, she untangled herself from Derrik and reached for it, noticing Brielle's name flashing on the screen.

"Hey, Bri," she answered, trying to mask her disappointment at the interruption.

"Desi! You forgot about our plans to take the boys into town today, didn't you?" Brielle teased, her voice tinged with amusement.

"Maybe," Desiree admitted with a sheepish grin, glancing at Derrik. "Time flies when you're having fun."

"You two just can't keep your hands off each other, can you?"

Desiree felt herself blush. "We got a little distracted. But we'll be right down, I promise."

"Uh huh, I'm sure you did," Brielle teased. "Hurry up, the boys are ready and so are we. No more practicing!"

"Okay, okay, see you in a minute." Desiree hung up and turned to Derrik. "I guess we should get moving. Everybody's waiting on us."

"We can pick up where we left off later," he murmured before pressing a lingering kiss to her lips before reluctantly sliding out of bed.

Desiree hurriedly showered and threw on a sweater and pair of jeans, quickly running a brush through her tangled hair. As they prepared for their outing, Desiree couldn't help but feel a flutter of excitement. She looked forward to the day spent with her family and friends, knowing the secret she carried served as a reminder of the strength of their bond, a promise of the joy yet to come.

.. ⊷ ..

Desiree and Derrik, along with their friends and his sister, arrived at the bustling amusement park in the center of downtown Breckinridge. The crisp winter air was filled with the sounds of laughter, music, and the mechanized whirs of the rides. The winter sun cast a soft glow on the streets, illuminating the quaint storefronts and twinkling fairy lights that adorned every lamppost. The enchanting ambiance was only heightened by the distant sound of laughter and thrill-seekers at the amusement park nearby. A surge of excitement bubbled up within Desiree as she walked along the sidewalk, hand-in-hand with Derrik and their two sons.

"Look, Mommy!" Dylan exclaimed, pointing to the carousel of horses. His eyes sparkled with anticipation, his small body quivering with energy.

"Wow, that looks like so much fun," Desiree acknowledged. "Do you want to ride?"

"Can we please! Mommy, I wanna ride." Dylan and Dykota voices echoed together.

She turned to Derrik, giving him a look.

He grinned, tipping his head. "Aye, Justin let's take the boys for a ride."

"I bet I can beat you there!" Justin called out, scooping up Dylan in his arms and taking off, leaving a confused Derrik behind.

Dykota tugged on his pants leg. "C'mon, Daddy! Pick me up too!"

"Hey, you cheated! Wait for us!" Derrik swept Dykota up into his arms and ran to catch up with Justin and Dylan.

"Look at them acting like little boys." Brielle remarked, rolling her eyes playfully.

Jayde laughed pointing. "Especially that overgrown one named Derrik. You see he ain't trying to lose."

"I know y'all better not drop my babies!" Desiree yelled after them.

"Oh, they know better." Brielle reassured her but didn't hide the threat in her tone.

Jayde responded, nodding in agreement. "Right, 'cause trust me, Derrik will catch these hands if he drops my Kota."

A smile reached Desiree's ears. She took notice of how effortlessly Brielle and Jayde seemed to be bonding with each other. It warmed her heart to see her best friend and sister-in-law getting along so well.

"Hey, I wanted to talk to y'all about something." Desiree glanced at the carousel where Derrik and Justin were getting the boys settled onto the ride before swinging her attention back to Brielle and Jayde. They both nodded, their expressions turning serious. "It's about Janelle and her unexpected guest."

"You mean Elle and her BFF, Khloe." Brielle replied with an air of sarcasm.

Desiree rolled her eyes. "Yeah. Her showing up has me wondering how the rest of this vacation is going to play out. I feel like she's up to something."

"Me too," Jayde admitted, her brow furrowing with concern. "She's my cousin, but Janelle's been unpredictable. I can honestly say ever since her mom died, she's been acting out. Ain't no telling what her ass might pull especially if she starts drinking."

Brielle glanced at Desiree briefly before she chimed in. Her voice was firm while she cautioned. "Well, cousin or not, for everyone's sake she needs to check her friend. So long as Khloe keeps her distance from Desi, we're good."

"Exactly," Desiree nodded. "I just want us to be on the same page in case anything happens."

Reaching out for Desiree's hand, Jayde affirmed. "Even though that's my first cousin, you're my big sister now. I'm going to make sure nothing happens."

Pointing her index finger directly at Desiree, Brielle proclaimed with conviction, "Listen, Khloe won't mess with that one right there. Or else she will relive what happened that day in your brother's house." Her eyes were determined and unyielding.

Desiree winked at her best friend with a big grin and blurted out. "Knuck if you buck!"

"Bitch, think I won't!" Brielle purse her lips.

Jayde clapped in amusement. "When Derrik told me about it, I died laughing. I wished I was a fly on the wall. But that's why I don't understand her being here. Okay, her mother passed away. I get it that's something she and Khloe bonded over. Even so, I could never show my face again. Talk about being thirsty as fuck."

"That part! But clearly, she's trying to prove a point that none of us cares about. So what, you got a fiancé. Doesn't change what your trifling ass did. All that scheming for money and a man that didn't even want your silly ass. No, I couldn't show my face either." Brielle waved her hands, shaking her head.

Desiree couldn't agree more. It didn't make sense Khloe's reasons for wanting to be there. Yet, she was there subjecting herself to be in the presence of her former lover and his family. Desiree turned her head to focus on her husband. Derrik and the boys were still on the carousel, grinning from ear to ear. Her heart swelled as she watched them—it reminded her that no matter how difficult things might get, their love would always overpower any adversity thrown their way.

Once the boys finished their third time around the carousel, they made their way through the amusement park, delighting in each attraction. Derrik hoisted one of the twins onto his shoulders while Justin took the other, both men forming a makeshift train for them to ride. The boys squealed with glee, reaching out to touch the colorful decorations that adorned the lively park.

Suddenly, the nausea hit her like a freight train. "Gimme a minute, I need to use the restroom," Desiree announced.

She didn't stop when she heard Derrik asking if she wanted to take the boys with her. She couldn't. Her stomach roiled, threatening to spew the contents from their breakfast. Thankfully she'd remembered they passed the building some feet behind. She quickly stumbled inside to the last stall just as the bile rose to her mouth. Desiree clung to the side of the toilet, retching repeatedly. She overheard someone calling out to check on her, but she could barely muster a feeble groan.

"Heh, those twists and turns get me every time too. Take it easy, hun."

"Mmhmm."

After a few minutes, Desiree started to feel a bit better. She was drained and exhausted from the vomiting. It had taken all the energy out of her body. She finished brushing her teeth, glanced in the reflection of the mirror, and knew she wouldn't be able to hide it from Derrik that something was wrong. Dammit, you really are being a little princess in there. Desiree thought to herself, turning on the faucet. She grabbed some paper towels from the holder and soaked them in the cool water. Once they were saturated, she placed the compress on her neck for comfort and to lower her body temperature.

There was a lounge chair for nursing mothers in the waiting area of the restroom. Desiree sat for a few moments to gather her composure after the morning sickness episode. It took ten more minutes before she finally exited the restroom and stepped out to everyone standing in front of the building.

"There's Mommy!" Dylan shouted.

Dykota bolted over to her with his arms outstretched. "Mommy! Mommy!"

"My Kota bear, come here." She picked him up once he reached her. Desiree nuzzled his neck eliciting a high-pitched squeal from him.

"Mommy you tickle me!"

"Baby girl, you good? I was about to come in there."

Brielle jokingly. "Oh god no. I'm glad you didn't. 'Cause we would've been out here waiting forever with y'all nasty selves. Can't have no bathroom around y'all in peace."

Desiree felt the heat creeping into her cheeks when Derrik's gaze met hers. Stifling a giggle, she buried her face in Dykota's neck. Her best friend wasn't exaggerating—she and Derrik seemed to have an unspoken agreement that bathrooms needed to be 'christened' by them.

"Family!"

Everyone's attention went to the voice coming from the opposite direction. It was Janelle waving energetically at them.

"Oh my gosh! What are the odds running into y'all here!"

"Really, Janelle? Do you have to be fake?" Jayde asked without hiding her annoyance. "I know my mom told you where we were."

"Okay, yeah, Auntie O did mention we might run into y'all." Janelle lifted her shoulders in a slight shrug. "But this place is huge. I didn't think it was possible, but hey, here we are. What are y'all doing?"

Desiree exchanged glances with Derrik. She'd hoped with her eyes she covertly signaled that they wouldn't be doing anything with them.

"How about we go hit the racetrack and do the go karts!" Janelle suggested enthusiastically, her eyes sparkling with devious excitement. She turned and pointed in the other direction of the park. "We saw it over there."

Khloe stood beside Janelle, a smile playing at the corners of her lips. She then spoke directly to Derrik. "My belov—uhh Derrik, I remember you used to love going to Andretti's."

No, this bitch didn't. Desiree placed Dykota on the ground. Her eyes bounced back and forth between Derrik and Khloe. Derrik gave her subtle negative gesture in response. She could feel the muscles in her face twitching more than the heat radiating in her ears.

Derrik haughtily snorted. While he spoke, his eyes never met Khloe's. They were trained on Desiree. "Yeah, you're right I used to." He edged toward Desiree and draped a protective arm around her shoulder. He glanced down at their sons and then fixed his gaze on Desiree. "But I haven't been since the boys were born since they're too little to ride."

Janelle refuted. "But there's stuff over there for them to do. Come on, it'll be fun. Don't be a kill joy, Charlie Brown!"

Derrik glared at Janelle, his tone was firm and stern. "Did you hear what I just said? If they can't get on, I'm not riding. Anyway, we've been here all day. I know the boys are getting pretty tired. We still have some other spots we wanted to hit in here. Then we're heading back."

Desiree peered down at their sons. They showed no signs of fatigue. Their eyes were wide with curiosity and excitement. However, she understood his intention was to keep her from being put in an awkward situation with Khloe and prevent any potential drama between them.

"That was the itinerary right, baby girl?" Derrik asked, his warm hand resting on the small of her back.

Desiree smirked and shot him a wink. "Why yes, my beloved it has been rather a long day. They need their rest. And we still need time to finish what we started."

"Here they go again." Brielle groaned playfully.

Justin and Jayde teasingly made exasperated sounds.

"Forget them. That's the plan, and it sounds good to me." Derrik tugged her closer and planted a quick, reassuring kiss on her lips.

Dykota let out a squeal of delight while pointing. "Ooooh Daddy kissing Mommy!"

"Boy what did I tell you? Mommy is mine so I can kiss her."

He pouted. "But she's mine too. Can I kiss her?"

"Of course, you can, Kota."

"Me too, Mommy!" Dylan whined.

"Elle, I'll be over there." Khloe blurted out and walked away without waiting for Janelle to respond.

Before kneeling down to her boys, Desiree watched Khloe roll her eyes, spin around, and storm away. She couldn't hold back from laughing when Jayde waved goodbye.

"Okay see you later, Khloe! Elle, I guess you better get going. Your girl looks like she still wants to go do them karts."

Janelle shrugged. "A'ight that's y'all's loss. Catch y'all back at the house!"

Derrik flashed Desiree a devious grin. "Y'all have fun!"

"Petty LaBelle, you just had to bring out your shady boots. Why yes, my beloved it has been a rather long day. Now you know beloved was her nickname for Derrik. And the kissing with the boys chiming in. Your girl is thirty-eight hot! You can see the steam coming out of her ears. Look." Brielle pointed.

Desiree twisted her head in the opposite direction where Khloe had gone. In that moment, Khloe turned around and locked eyes with her. It was unmistakable. The resentment and rage in Khloe's stare felt like a searing flame to Desiree. She rose to her feet, never breaking eye contact, and moved closer to Derrik, who instinctively wrapped his arm around her. He pressed a kiss on top of her head. Desiree's amber eyes returned the fiercest warning to Khloe as she mouthed one word: "Mine.

CHAPTER 6

Derrik locked eyes with her, watching her hazel eyes roll back as he buried himself to the hilt. Withdrawing slowly from her warm throbbing core, he peered down momentarily. The sight of her secretions covering the length of his shaft made him even harder. He moistened his thumb with saliva and moved it in a circular pattern around her love button. At the same time, Derrik dipped lower in his stance, thrust his hips upward, and sank deep into her hot pocket. Desiree opened her mouth, threatening to cry out. Derrik's lips sealed over hers, muffling the sound. He rocked his hips in a steady rhythm, thrusting into her with each stroke. Their kiss vibrated with her moans of pleasure. She beat against his chest right as her pussy clamped down on his dick. Then she released, instantly turning her fiery furnace into a juice box. Even with both the faucet water running and the humming of the ceiling fan in the background, Derrik could still hear the squelching sounds of their lovemaking, coaxing him to chase after his own nut. Just as the familiar sensation crept into his abdomen a loud banging noise rapped against the bathroom door.

Although startled, he couldn't stop mid-stroke. His orgasm was so close. Right there. Derrik reached up and covered Desiree's mouth. He pistoned faster until he emptied his nuts. Letting his head drop, he growled against her breast. "Fffuck!

Brielle's voice came from the other side. "Ugh, dammit, you two! We've been in there waiting to get these games started. It don't take both of y'all to check on them babies. I should've known when you said you were coming to check on her what you would end up doing." She continued in an annoyed, yet jesting tone. "Seriously, the bathroom

176

that we all gotta use? Hurry up! Or else I'm sending Uncle Vic and your dad!"

He peeked up at Desiree who had a satisfied grin on her face. Derrik flashed her the same before sharing a quick kiss.

"Damn, baby girl. That quickie took longer than I expected."

"Because there are no quickies with you, Derrik."

"You're right. And seeing you leak all over this sink, my dick getting hard again. I think I can cut it to five minutes. Let me slide in real quick."

Desiree shook her head and playfully pushed him away. "Nah uh, 'cause you know Bri ain't lying. She'll send your crazy ass uncle and then everybody will be clowning us."

"Think I care?" he asked while helping her down from the counter.

"Oh, I know you don't. That's how I ended up like an Auntie Anne's pretzel up there a few minutes ago."

Derrik let out a hearty laugh, smacking her on the ass. In a hurry, both worked to clean up from their shameless bathroom tryst. A few minutes later, he ushered them into the game room, allowing Desiree to walk in before him. Voices filled the air with joy and conversation as they stepped inside. He glanced down at Desiree who lowered her eyes, blushing profusely with a sheepish grin. She made her way over to one side of the room, her cheeks glowing an embarrassed red as her best friend and sister-in-law welcomed her with laughing and snickering. He swung his attention to the other side of the game room.

His dad, Vance, sat at the head of the oval-shaped poker table, large enough to accommodate ten players. His eyes sparkled as he exchanged playful banter with Uncle Vic, who was shuffling the deck of cards with practiced ease. Hodges, his reserved, yet observant bodyguard, grinned at the jesting passing between his dad and uncle. Desiree's dad, David, gave a pleasant smile as he reclined in his chair, his hazel eyes twinkling with amusement. Brielle's boyfriend, Justin, sat next to David, with a wide smile stretching across his face. He too seemed to enjoy their verbal sparring.

As soon as Derrik and his father made eye contact, Vance let out a hearty chuckle. "Ah, there he goes! We were just talking about dealing a quick hand so I could shut Vic up."

Uncle Vic snorted loudly. "I know you ain't talking 'bout me. Hodge already got a tight lip so you ain't gotta worry 'bout him. You must be talking 'bout Dave or Justin over there. But you wasn't gon' shut me up."

Hodges grumbled while the brothers continued in an animated debate about who would've emerged victorious from the hand. David and Justin added their two cents, claiming they would have done their best not to be defeated.

"C'mon, Pops. How you gon' start without me? You know I had to make sure the twins were asleep," Derrik lied, pulling up a chair and taking his place at the table. He quickly looked across the room meeting Desiree's narrowed gaze at his obvious lie. He shot her a sly wink.

His dad waved a hand. "Hmph, you was taking too long. We tryna to win some money up in here. Right fellas?"

Everyone at the table bobbed their heads in agreement to his dad's question. He was about to speak up, but his uncle beat him to it.

"And now that everybody's here it's time to get this game going," Uncle Vic announced as he began dealing the cards.

Once getting all his cards, Derrik picked them up. He studied them carefully while attempting to gauge the others' reactions to their hands. He knew his dad and uncle were seasoned poker players, but this didn't stop him from feeling a surge of competitiveness.

"Okay it's been a minute since you played against me, Derrik. I hope you're ready to come up off that bread, son." his dad teased.

"I don't think so." Derrik responded with a grin, feeling the familiar thrill of friendly rivalry. "But I'm not just playing against you, Pops. I've got my eyes on everyone at this table especially Uncle Vic."

"Aye, watch yo mouth, nephew. I taught you everything I know."

"Exactly the reason why I've got to keep my eyes on you."

Uncle Vic chuckled. "Heh, touché but you right. I would too."

As the game progressed there were outbursts of bantering between the men and lighthearted teasing. Although Derrik should've been paying attention to what he was doing, so he wouldn't lose any money, his concentration was constantly drawn to Desiree. He could hear her laughter clearly from the other side of the game room.

Desiree urged in a playful tone. "You see what color is up. Let's go!"

"Shh, I'm tryna see what I wanna stack." Jayde brushed her hair away from her face, pulling it into a ponytail. She then shifted her gaze downward at the cards in her hand, seemingly deep in thought of her next move.

"Stop stalling, Jayde."

Brielle's eyes sparkled with mischief as she warned, "Don't rush her, Desi, 'cause you don't want this smoke."

Desiree responded by rotating her neck and waving away the concern with a jest, "Whatever, Bri. You better be glad what I got ain't coming your way."

"Keep talking diva. I got you as soon as Jayde get it together over there."

"Okay there. Geez!" Jayde dropped a stack of three cards with the number 9.

Brielle quickly followed up with two Draw Four cards. "Ha! Now pick 'em up, diva!"

"Bam!" Desiree slapped down two more Draw Four cards. "Let's see what you've got, Jayde."

Jayde groaned in mock despair as she began drawing sixteen cards from the deck. "But I'm supposed to be your sister!"

"Tuh! Ain't no family at this table! It's every woman for themselves." Desiree let out a maniacal laugh.

"Don't get too happy 'cause I ain't going down without a fight. My mama 'nem ain't raise no punk."

"Girl, how are you doing all that talking with a hand full of cards?"

"Just let me get this hand together. And you better hope we don't reverse this table 'cause it's on then, sister!"

Desiree changed the octave in her voice to sound like Katt Williams and taunted holding up the few cards left in her hand. "Don't worry, I'll wait."

"Oh my god, Derrik your wife is ruthless!" Jayde rolled her eyes jokingly.

He was about to respond when Janelle sauntered into the room. She was followed by Khloe and two unknown men. Standing tall enough to almost reach the doorway, the first man had brown skin and a curly top fade. He wore snow-covered Timberland boots, blue jeans, and a burgundy shirt that made him stand out from the other guy. The second man was a bit shorter and had a darker complexion. He wore a white shirt and dark blue jeans, along with an orange flat cap and a green scarf. In an instant, the atmosphere transformed from joyous to unsettling, leaving Derrik with a sense of unease that he couldn't quite pinpoint.

"Look who finally made it!" Janelle hiccupped and announced with a wide grin, seemingly oblivious to the change in mood. "Family, this is Khloe's fiancé, Bakari Woods, and his friend Terrance Mack. I told y'all they were coming. They couldn't wait to meet y'all and join in on the festivities!"

"Is that so?" Brielle leaned back in her chair, not quite masking the edge in her voice.

"Peaches." Justin cautioned with a stern look.

"What babe? I'm just asking. She said they couldn't wait to meet us. Pshh, yeah right. Who are we? More like they couldn't wait to meet the Carters."

Derrik got up from the table, his protective instincts on high alert. He winked and gave Desiree a reassuring smile. The anxiety etched onto her face when the men entered the room was not lost on him. Turning his attention to his sister, Derrik watched her with concern. Jayde gave a brief nod, her gaze bouncing between the new people and him. After giving a covert signal to Hodges, Derrik moved over to where his cousin stood with their new guests and cleared his throat. "Hey, what's up? How y'all doing? I'm Derrik Carter."

Bakari stepped forward. "Yeah, we know who you are. Kinda hard not to considering you're the CEO of BlakBeatz. Nice to finally meet, though." His voice was sharp and his squinted gaze cold as he scanned Derrik up and down. He then extended a hand toward him.

The hostility in his voice was unmistakable. Derrik could've sworn he saw something wild brewing in Bakari's eyes for a split second. He quickly shook the other man's hand, then stepped back deciding not to pursue whatever was threateningly unspoken between them.

Instead, after exchanging a quick handshake with Terrance, he made a brief introduction of everyone in the room before taking a seat back at the table. Derrik was acutely aware of his dad's attentive eyes as the situation unfolded between their guests. He subtly nodded in Hodges's direction, letting him know that everything would be okay, so long as Bakari stayed in his place. He had no intention of allowing any of it to escalate to violence.

"Hey, where's Auntie O and Ms. Nita? I wanted them to meet Bakari and Terrance too."

Derrik had to struggle to keep his face expressionless, almost succumbing to the temptation of a sarcastic response. His dad's words saved him from it.

"They were out for some last-minute shopping and then they had to get groceries for the holiday brunch. After being out of the house all day, they wanted to rest," Vance stated matter-of-factly before shifting his gaze to Derrik.

Derrik stayed silent and his face remained neutral. He rotated his neck to glance at Janelle when she replied.

She nodded in understanding but, her voice deflated, "Oh okay. I guess y'all will get to meet them tomorrow then."

"Well, thanks for the warm welcome," Bakari replied, with a confident smirk. His eyes lingered on Derrik for a moment before moving to the poker table. "Mind if we join?"

"Of course, they don't!" Despite the tension that had taken hold of the room, Janelle's voice was full of enthusiasm. She directed her question to Uncle Vic. "There's plenty of room at the table and the more, the merrier right, Daddy?"

Derrik sighed inwardly. As much as he wanted to keep his distance from Bakari, he couldn't outright refuse to include them in the game without coming across as rude. Before Derrik could respond either way, Uncle Vic gestured toward the table. "If they wanna lose their money, hell yeah. Pull up a chair."

Janelle addressed Bakari and Terrance, her eyes sparkling with mischief. "I'm sure they could use some fresh competition."

"Oh, I'm all for that as long as nobody gets in their feelings." Bakari said in a dry, mocking tone as he looked at Derrik.

Derrik narrowed his eyes. He could tell the guy was trying to goad him into saying or doing something stupid. Bakari and Terrance sat down, trading glances between him and Hodges. Derrik knew how to keep his cool. However, if it came down to it, he would flip the table over to handle business. While Uncle Vic dealt out the poker chips and explained their rules, Derrik remained quiet watching their reactions.

The moment his uncle finished, his dad rubbed his hands together in anticipation. "Alright, gentlemen, let's get this game going."

The conversation and jesting started up again, with chip stacks and cards passing quickly between them as they placed their bets. Derrik found himself exchanging friendly jabs with his dad, uncle, father-in-law, and Justin like they'd done earlier before the new guys came. His smile faded when he saw Bakari looking in his direction.

"Your poker face might need to improve, Derrik." Uncle Vic teased, causing the others to chuckle. He showed his hand and leaned back with a smug grin.

"Speak for yourself," Derrik shot back, refocusing his eyes on the cards in his hand. He grinned, revealing that he had the winning hand. "I don't know why he keeps thinking I didn't learn from the best."

"Ahh damn, nephew. This is what we're doing?"

"Yep, now gimme my money ol' man."

"I know I'm not trying to explain to Nita how I lost all this money to our rich son-in-law." David muttered as he tossed his losing cards onto the table.

Vance nodded with a groan. "At least you ain't gotta explain it to his mama how her son took their vacation fund."

Derrik's eyes went wide. "No way Pops! I know you didn't," he exclaimed.

Vance laughed and simply nodded. "I most certainly did, but I know you got me and Dave."

Derrik cracked a smile. His dad was right. No matter how much they lost to him, or how much money they owed him, in the end he'd make sure neither of them had to pay a penny. His dad shuffled the cards and dealt the next hand.

"Full house," Uncle Vic announced proudly, spreading his cards out on the table for all to see. "Now gimme my money!"

Derrik teased, "About time, Unc."

The other men groaned and threw their cards at him in mock annoyance.

A couple of games later the atmosphere shifted when Bakari and Terrance started playing more aggressively. Their betting style and smug expressions added another undercurrent of tension to the game. Derrik couldn't shake the feeling that Bakari was trying to prove something, perhaps even attempting to assert dominance over him.

"Nice hand," Bakari commented, offering a tight smile as he slapped his hand down and began scooping up his winnings. "But I think I've got you beat this time, Derrik."

Derrik forced a congenial smile, but his thoughts were racing. Why is he trying so hard to get under my skin? I hope he isn't doing this behind Khloe.

"Your deal, Derrik," Vance called out, snapping his attention back to the table.

Derrik shuffled the cards and dealt them out, his fingers moving deftly over the worn deck. As much as he tried to focus on the game and conversations around him, it was impossible to ignore Bakari's penetrating gaze. Clenching his jaw, Derrik placed his cards face down on the table. For a split second he peered over at Hodges exchanging a knowing look. Derrik looked around the table before focusing on Bakari's serious expression. For a brief moment, their gazes met. The intensity of their eye contact lasted a few seconds longer than Derrik would've liked. When he finally spoke, his tone commanded the attention of everyone in the room. "Yo, my man you got a problem?"

Immediately the room went quiet. Bakari threw his hand down and flexed his jaw. "Nah, my man. Do you?"

Derrik scoffed, "I know this nig—you can't be seri ... nah you know what." He shoved his chair back, rising to his feet and Hodges did the same. Derrik marched over to the table where his cousin, Janelle and Khloe sat. Out of the corner of his eye, he saw that Bakari and his friend had also stood from their seats. He'd tried, but he no longer had any need to be civil about it.

"Janelle this is the bullshit I was talking about! I don't give a fuck about what happened with her! You could've consoled her ass on FaceTime. But no, you wanted to bring her here around my wife! Then you got her man in my house trying to flex. He don't really want it 'cause 'tis the season for giving somebody a beatdown. Nah, they gotta go. Not tomorrow. Tonight. Right now." Derrik's eyes burned with fury as he glared at Khloe. He whipped his head around to face Bakari, nostrils flaring. "Yo, my man, get your girl and get the fuck out!"

"Derrik!" Janelle gasped. She rushed to her feet. "You-you can't be serious?"

"Do it look like I'm laughing, Janelle. You wanted to be her support right now, heh? Well, your ass can leave with them too!" Derrik shouted before he stepped back from her and extended a hand to Desiree.

His cousin pleaded desperately. "Daddy, Uncle Van please talk to him."

Derrik kept his gaze fixed on Bakari as the room erupted with rising voices. Janelle continued with begging his dad and uncle to intervene and persuade him to reconsider, while Bakari and Khloe exchanged heated words about it being an ambush for him coming to her ex-boyfriend's house.

"Ex-boyfriend?" Desiree and Brielle said at the time.

"Bruh. This shit just gets better," Derrik mumbled, shaking his head in disbelief. Before he could even refute that lie, his wife handled it, swiftly fact checking Bakari.

"She wishes." Desiree let out a dismissive snort, "For seven years she was his jumpoff. That's it, that's all."

Khloe glared at Desiree, but she didn't respond.

Brielle chortled, "Wait, so Khloe, you had him thinking it was more? Derrik ain't want your ass then and he don't care about you being engaged to nobody else girl!"

"Hey, what is going on down here?"

It was his mom, Olivia that'd entered the game room. Desiree's mom, Juanita was right on her heels, yawning and rubbing her eyes. Vance and David quickly went over to them.

Derrik threw his thumb in Janelle's direction. "Your niece and her messy behavior as usual. But you agreed to this, Ma. I'm sorry but Khloe gets no empathy from me, especially not now. Her man came up in here acting like we got beef. Over her? Pfft! Nah, they gots to go. And Janelle can take her ass on too!"

Olivia gasped, "Derrik!" Her gaze bounced from Khloe to Janelle. She furrowed her brow and started to open her mouth, but Derrik wasn't about to sway his decision or let her lecture him on how to handle the matter.

"No, Ma. Don't let them sad eyes or the circumstances fool you. You weren't down here. Dad and Uncle Vic can explain it because I'm done talking about it. I'm not okay with what just went down and I'm not dealing with it." He folded his arms across his chest.

Derrik then watched as his dad and uncle talked with his mom and Janelle. It soon became clear they wouldn't be able to sway his decision. Janelle began leading Khloe, Bakari, and Terrance from the room. She paused for a moment, looking back at Derrik regretfully, but he was unmoved by her silent plea. His cousin foolishly thought it wouldn't be an issue. Yet, he knew she loved being an orchestrator of chaos and was down to see some kind of drama pop off. He certainly wasn't going to lessen the feeling nor overlook that Khloe was at the heart of it all. Derrik refused to let her off easy.

Once they were gone, Derrik took Desiree's hand and led her over to the seating area with the sofa and lounge chairs. After sitting in one of the accent chairs, he pulled her onto his lap. Squeezing her close, he apologized for losing his temper. "But I knew something like this would happen. The moment he walked in I could feel his energy was off. He kept shooting dirty looks. Then he came out his mouth reckless. Nah, I wasn't about to let that shit slide. And I don't know what those two were thinking, but yeah, they set ol' boy up."

"No need to apologize, babe. I know you would've avoided it if you could," Desiree said reassuringly. "And they sure did set his ass up. The thing is, they weren't thinking."

"Khloe must've had a lapse in her memory because she really tried it. Loss of your mom or not, just no," Brielle chimed in as she walked up.

Jayde added, "This whole thing was a big no."

Brielle, Justin, and Jayde took up seating on the sofa and loveseat next to them. They continued chatting about the events of the night unfolding, showing their solidarity with Derrik's decision telling the unwanted guests to leave. His parents along with Desiree's parents, and Uncle Vic also joined them in the seating area. While everyone else sat down, his dad came up to him.

Vance let out an audible sigh. "Son, I just wanted to say you did a good job on keeping your head."

"A better job than me that's for damn sure." Uncle Vic interjected.

Vance nodded in agreement. "Yeah, we saw how the young man was talking. We told Liv and Nita he was trying to egg you on. You did right in asking them to leave."

"They weren't going to be in here with that energy ruining the holiday for the rest of us." Derrik continued in a reassuring tone, "I wasn't about to let that happen."

Uncle Vic rocked his head back and forth. "I know Janelle ain't want this to happen. She couldn't even tell us why she thought it was okay to invite them other than she wanted to be there since that girl's mama passed away. Even so, that doesn't mean—"

"They can't leave! None of us can!" Janelle burst into the game room, her eyes wide with panic.

Hodges rushed in after her, motioning for the door. "Boss, you need to see this."

Derrik was already trying to process Janelle's initial statement when the next words out of her mouth meant his patience would likely be tested in the days to come.

"There's a storm coming! And we're already snowed in!"

CHAPTER 7

The snowstorm roared outside, vicious gusts of wind rattled the windows, as if nature itself were trying to claw its way into the luxury cabin. Large white flakes swirled madly through the dark skies, piling on the ground, and blocking off any chance of escape. It'd been like that since the night before and throughout the day. With Christmas Eve just a day away, Derrik couldn't believe that instead of twinkling lights and joyful celebrations, they were stuck inside their holiday retreat.

"Boss, everything's good. The generator's full of gas in case the power goes out," Hodges said as he placed the last pile of firewood next to the fireplace.

Derrik nodded but didn't look up. He was too busy scrolling through his phone looking at the reports from the surrounding areas impacted by the snowstorm. He'd been keeping a watchful eye once the storm hit Colorado the night before. Although he'd heard about it, the weathermen claimed it was going to pass over their area. That'd been a lie. They were now trapped on a side of the mountain more than forty-five minutes away from the town. The city's snow-removal crew wouldn't make it out to his family until after the storm passed and all the roads in town were cleared. It would be a few days before they got to them.

"Of all the days for this to happen," Olivia mumbled.

"Well Liv, Mother Nature's got a wicked sense of humor," Vance, added with a cynical chuckle.

"Nothing's funny about what we'll have to deal with these next couple of days especially if ..." her voice trailed off.

189

Derrik peeked up, meeting his mother's concerned gaze. He knew what she meant—she didn't have to finish her sentence. After the unfortunate news that they were all stuck together, Derrik made it clear to Janelle to keep her guests on the other side of the house away from him. The fewer interactions between them, the better. He diverted his eyes away from her and went back to his phone searching for any updates on when the storm was expected to end.

"I would like to try and get some rest," Olivia said softly. "Hopefully it looks better out there in the morning."

"Alright son, we're gonna call it a night." Then Vance spoke to Desiree's parents who were relaxing in the recliners a few feet away from them. "Dave, Nita, we'll catch up with y'all in the morning."

The two of them gave subtle nods to acknowledge his parents. Shortly after they left, her parents rose from their seats, announcing they too were heading upstairs for the evening. They offered to take the boys up to the nursery since they'd fallen asleep in Desiree's arms. Her mom removed Dykota from her lap while her dad gently lifted Dylan from her side.

Desiree rose from the sofa to walk them out. "Thank you. Have a good night."

"Thanks, Pumpkin. You too." He planted a kiss on her forehead and stepped back looking around the room. "Hope you all sleep well," her dad called out as he left the room, his voice barely audible above the howling wind.

Uncle Vic decided to hang around for a little while longer. He went over to the L-shaped bar in the corner where Hodges was now sitting. After pulling out a few bottles, he offered, "Should I pour for anybody else? Hell, it looks like we all could use a shot."

"Nah, I'm good, Unc," Derrik said barely bringing his eyes up from his phone.

"What about you, Justin my boy? You gon' leave Unc hanging?"

Rising to his feet, Justin outstretched a hand in Brielle's direction. He shook his head with regret in his voice. "Unfortunately, Unc this time I'mma have to. Me and Peaches about to take it down too. She just said her head was starting to hurt. We'll see y'all in the morning."

"Feel better, diva." Desiree shared a quick hug with her best friend. She was about to sit down next to Derrik when Uncle Vic held up a glass. "Nope, none for me. I don't do brown, and I know you're not making lemon drops the way Bri does."

"You got that right. Welp, I guess it's just you and me, Hodg." Uncle Vic started pouring cognac in a glass.

Janelle came stumbling into the room. "Daddy, you can go 'head and pour one for me!"

"Uhh maybe you should slow down, especially since you're already three sheets to the wind," Jayde quipped.

After taking the shot glass from her dad, Janelle put a hand up in Jayde's direction. "Why don't you mind your business? I can handle myself, thank you very much. Maybe if you drink a lil' you won't be so uptight. Or perhaps you need some dick in your life."

"Watch your mouth, Janelle," Uncle Vic chided as he shook his head.

Janelle ignored her dad and set the glass down on the bar countertop. She narrowed her eyes as she walked toward Jayde, clearly focused on confronting her. "At least I see one of y'all is finally getting some. Kudos to Jordy."

"Hmm, what gave you the impression that I don't?" Jayde rolled her eyes and snorted. "Trust that I get plenty of it. But you, goodness, you're such an embarrassment to a man if he did want you. Does this guy Terrance know you're a drunk?"

"A drunk? You think because I come around tipsy sometimes that I'm an alcoholic? Ha! Girl bye."

"I never called you an alcoholic but hey you're starting to show the signs, cuz. I guess we should call it how we see it."

"Hey, what the hell is going on?" Uncle Vic came from behind the bar.

At the same time, Desiree tugged on Derrik's arm getting his attention. He set his phone down on the end table and got to his feet, waving his uncle off. "I got it Unc." Derrik moved where his cousin and sister were squaring off in the middle of the room. "Aye, knock it the fuck off. Janelle, why don't you go take a nap."

She scoffed, her face reddening with anger. "Wow, here we fucking go. See what I mean, Daddy. I told you Uncle Van's kids really think they're the shit."

"You said it, not me," Jayde declared, pointing an accusing finger. "Something's obviously bothering you. It seems like you have a problem. Let's hear it."

"Y'all think you're so much better than me, don't you?" Janelle spat with a tone full of bitterness. "From Derrik to you and your sister—always looking down on me like I'm some kind of ... of charity case!"

"Janelle," Derrik started, in an attempt to calm her down, but she cut him off.

"No, Derrik! 'Cause I've had enough!" Janelle's voice trembled and tears threatened to spill from her eyes. "I lost my mom, and I had nobody. My dad was there, sure, but I needed my cousins. Instead of being there for me like I thought you would be, all y'all did was judge me! Me! I thought we were family!"

"Janelle, you know it wasn't like that," Jayde attempted reasoning with her. "We all missed Aunt Athena, and we did want to be there for you. We tried. But sometimes, it was hard to know how. We didn't know what you needed or what to say. You pushed us away most of the time."

"Bullshit! I didn't push you away! You pushed me away! Did you bother to ask? No! And you could've helped by treating me like an equal, not like some screw-up! You wanna know why I invited Khloe. She gets me, that's why."

Jayde argued, "So, you didn't care about how it would make your family feel bringing her here after what we all went through?"

"Fuck your feelings 'cause you don't care about mine." Janelle shouted back, her breath hitching in her throat.

"ENOUGH!" Derrik's voice boomed, silencing the room. His eyes bounced back and forth between his cousin and sister. In that moment, he could see the hurt hidden beneath Janelle's bravado, and his heart ached for her. "Janelle, you're right. We are family, and we should be there for each other. But that also means not tearing each other down. We need to find a way to come together. We need to fix this."

A bitter laugh escaped Janelle's lips, her gaze locked on the floor as she shook her head. "And what? You think you can fix everything, don't you, Derrik?" She glanced up at him, her tear ducts still pooling with unshed tears. "Well, some things aren't so easily mended."

"Girl, stop being so stubborn and listen to your cousin." Uncle Vic added, placing a hand on Janelle's shoulder. "We're all family here."

Jayde bit her lip. Derrik knew that she was just as desperate to resolve the conflict as he was. He gave his sister a pleading look hoping her words might help. Jayde whispered, her voice cracking. "Janelle, look I'm sorry, I didn't—"

Janelle put her hand in Jayde's face, "Save it." Then she pushed past Derrik and began marching out of the family room.

"Janelle!" Uncle Vic called after her, worry etched across his face. After a beat, he sighed heavily, casting Derrik a defeated look before chasing after Janelle.

Their once joyful holiday celebration had been reduced to a battlefield of hurt feelings and fractured relationships. Derrik knew he had to find a way to bridge the chasms that'd formed between them.

CHAPTER 8

The warm glow of Derrik's laptop screen was a stark contrast to the cold winter evening pressing against the windows. It was yet another day of the storm bringing blizzard-like conditions. The rich aroma of cinnamon and nutmeg wafted from the kitchen, mingling with the scent of the freshly cut fir tree in the living room. He heard the soft voices of his mom, and Desiree's mom, coming from the kitchen as they prepared dinner. The familiar cadence of their conversation provided a soothing background noise, helping him to concentrate on his tasks.

"JuaJua," Olivia's voice wavered slightly, "There's something I need to talk to you about."

Derrik tried not to eavesdrop, but the tone of his mom's voice pulled at his heartstrings. He couldn't help overhearing as his mom began to share her concerns.

"Of course, Liv. What's going on?"

"Remember I went for the biopsy last week. The results came back ... it's cancer."

Derrik's fingers froze above the keyboard, his entire body went rigid as tried to wrap his mind around his mom's words.

"Oh, Liv, I am so sorry. I know that wasn't what you wanted to hear." Juanita said softly. "What did the doctor say? What stage is it?"

"Stage two," Olivia replied, her voice breaking. "They want to start treatment right away, but I haven't told anyone yet. Not even Vance or the kids. I just ... I don't ... how do you tell your family something like that?"

"Liv, honey, you can't keep this a secret from your family. They need to know what you're going through."

194

Derrik sat in stunned silence, his mind racing with thoughts and emotions as he tried to process the news. His mom, the strong woman who had always been there for him, was facing one of the most challenging battles of her life. He felt a surge of protectiveness and love for her, along with an overwhelming sense of fear and helplessness. It was a conversation he never expected to overhear, and it shook him to his core.

"JuaJua, I'm so scared," Olivia whispered. "I don't want to burden my family with this, but I know I can't go through it alone."

"Liv, you are not a burden. You have a loving family who will stand by your side every step of the way. Including us. Let them and us help you fight this."

As Derrik listened, his heart pounded in his chest, as if trying to escape the suffocating grasp of the news he'd just overheard. Forgetting about work, he pushed himself up from the table. He stumbled out of the dining room, made his way down the hall and into the living room. His breathing grew shallow, and the room seemed to spin around him. He leaned against the partition arch for support.

"Pops ... it's Ma ... she-she has ... cancer." The words tumbled out of his mouth before he could stop them, the sound of his own voice echoing throughout the room. Instantly, all eyes turned to him, a collection of confusion and concern playing across their faces. Vance, set down the glass he was holding, the color draining from his face. Uncle Vic, always jovial, looked as though someone had knocked the wind out of him. Desiree got up from the sofa and rushed to his side.

"What did you just say, son?" Vance asked, his voice barely above a whisper.

"Ma said she has cancer," he repeated.

Desiree squeezed his arm tight. Her eyes were wide with alarm. "Derrik, what are you talking about?"

"I overheard her in the kitchen talking to your mom, baby girl."

"I didn't want you to find out like this," Olivia's voice trembled as she entered the living room, clutching Juanita's hand for support.

"Liv, why didn't you tell me?" Vance questioned, his voice thick with emotion as he approached her and wrapped his arm around her shoulders. He guided her over to the sofa.

"I'm so sorry," Olivia whispered. She looked up at her family gathered around her, sorrow mingling in her eyes.

"Mom, is it true?" Jayde, demanded, her brown eyes filled with shock and anger.

"Yes, sweetheart. I've been diagnosed with Stage two breast cancer."

Oblivious to the somber mood, Dylan giggled in delight. "Gammy O, you didn't say titty. Daddy, you didn't tell her she a good girl."

"Gammy O, you a good girl!" Dykota clapped.

She gave them a smile. "Thank you, babies."

Brielle and Justin offered to keep them distracted and quickly ushered the boys out of the room.

Once they were gone, Jayde asked in a small voice, voicing the question on Derrik's mind. "Why didn't you tell us?"

"Truthfully Jayde, sweetheart, I didn't want to ruin our time together," Olivia replied softly, tears glistening in her eyes. "And I didn't want to ruin Christmas."

Derrik moved to her side. Kneeling, he took her hand in both of his. "You could never ruin Christmas, Ma."

"He's right, Liv. You're the reason we do our Christmas vacation getaways. We couldn't do them without ..." Vance paused for a beat. He took his wife's hand squeezing it tight and spoke with conviction. "We're gonna face this together, my love. Every step of the way. We ain't going down without a fight."

Olivia gave a weak smile, her lower lip quivering as she tried to hold back the tears. "I know, Van. I know."

$$\cdot \cdot \infty \cdot \cdot$$

Derrik's heart ached as he observed his parents, knowing the difficult journey they were about to embark upon. He wished he could take it away, but all he could do was offer his love and support. "Hey, we're all in this together. Like Pops said, we'll be there too, every step of the way, no matter what."

"Ma, you're the strongest person I know," Jayde said, her voice full of admiration. "If anyone can beat this, it's you."

The family drew closer, forming a protective circle around Olivia. They shared solemn nods and tearful embraces, promising to be there for her through thick and thin. With everyone by his side committing themselves completely, Derrik could feel a strong determination developing inside of him. He knew what they faced ahead would be filled with challenges—endless medical treatments, sleepless nights spent worrying, and the constant presence of fear lurking in the background. They would do what they had to for his mom.

Derrik's voice was determined. "Ma, we're going to find the best doctors, explore every treatment option available, and fight this with everything we've got. We can and will overcome this."

"Thank you, my darlings. I know I can count on all of you," Olivia said softly. She rested her head on Vance's shoulder.

As they all stood around his mom, their emotions raw and exposed, Derrik felt a mixture of fear and resolve. This news had shaken them all to their core, but it was also bringing them closer together. No matter what challenges lay ahead, they would confront them as a united front, with love and support for one another.

CHAPTER 9

Desiree knelt on the cold tile floor, her head hovering over the toilet as another wave of nausea hit. She retched violently, emptying the meager contents of her stomach. When she was finished, she stood up on wobbly legs. She rinsed her mouth in the sink, catching a glimpse of her pale reflection in the mirror. A small smile formed on her lips. From everything she'd read during her first pregnancy, morning sickness was a good sign. It meant the baby—their baby—was growing healthy and strong. She splayed a hand on her stomach, excitement fluttering within. After trying for a while, she and Derrik were expecting again. She couldn't wait to see the look on his face when she finally told him the news. Taking a deep breath, Desiree straightened up and opened the bathroom door, only to nearly collide with Khloe. Her stomach churned unpleasantly as she regarded Derrik's former lover. Khloe's piercing brown eyes narrowed.

"Khloe," Desiree said icily, crossing her arms over her chest. "I didn't expect to see you."

"Why good morning, Desiree," Khloe replied, her voice dripping with forced sweetness. "You look ... radiant this morning."

The anger simmered in her chest, threatening to spill over. Instead of exchanging morning pleasantries, Desiree snapped abruptly, "What are you doing in here? What did my husband tell you?"

"I was just getting some water. Goodness, even with the fireplace it seems this house is so cold, don't you think?"

"You know what I think, Khloe, you're still hung up on Derrik." Desiree stepped closer and hissed, "Let's get one thing clear, Derrik is my husband. I won't have you prancing around here, thinking you still have a chance. Back off, or you'll regret it."

Khloe recoiled, shock registering on her face. Without giving her a chance to respond, Desiree walked away, head held high. She paused mid-stride and turned around. "Oh, and Khloe, let this be the last time we have this conversation," Desiree warned, her hazel eyes blazing with determination. With that, she turned on her heel, eager to find Derrik and share the news.

Desiree entered the family room, and a wave of warmth and comfort embraced her. The expansive space was adorned with twinkling lights that danced on the wooden walls, casting a soft glow over everybody in the room. An enormous Christmas tree stood proudly in the corner, its branches laden with shimmering ornaments and sparkling tinsel.

"Hey baby girl, we were wondering where you went. I was about to come and get you." Derrik called out.

Brielle chimed in teasingly, "No, you wasn't. I was because y'all would've taken too long."

"Sorry about that. I thought I'd forgotten a last present, but it's here." Desiree made her way over to Derrik. She sat next to him and pressed a gentle kiss to his lips.

"You feeling okay, baby girl?" Derrik questioned, his arm wrapping around her protectively.

"Much better now," she assured him, a soft smile playing on her lips as she thought about the secret that would soon be shared with everyone in the room.

Their boys sat on the opposite side of him, in between his parents, Olivia and Vance, who were engaged in an animated conversation with her parents. Uncle Vic sat nearby with Justin recounting one of his legendary stories. Laughter filled the room as they listened intently, their faces glowing with amusement.

Jayde and Brielle were over at the wet bar working together to get everyone a drink. Jayde came from behind the counter gracefully balancing a tray of champagne flutes filled with freshly prepared mimosas. "Alright, everyone! Let's have a toast to Christmas and being together."

Brielle handed her a glass, winked, and hush whispered, "Don't think I'd let you drink with precious cargo on board, diva."

Desiree smiled, thankful for her best friend looking out for her.

"Here's to the love and warmth of family. May we cherish these moments together, now and always." Jayde declared, raising her glass high.

"Cheers!" Everyone chorused, their voices melding together in a symphony of joy and celebration.

Derrik clapped his hands. "Alright, who's ready to open some presents?"

"Me!" The boys jumped up and down in excitement.

While his parents and hers helped with getting their sons' gifts, everyone else grabbed the different presents from under the tree with their names on them. Desiree approached Derrik and handed him a white rectangle-shaped box wrapped in a pink ribbon.

"Babe, this is something I didn't plan to give you, but once I saw it, I knew it would be the one thing you'd likely be most excited about receiving."

Derrik's brows pinched together as he looked down at the box in his hand and then back up at her.

"Go ahead and open it."

He pulled the pink ribbon from the white box. Before opening it, he glanced up at her again, a puzzled expression covering his face. Desiree nodded, encouraging him to keep going. Derrik lifted the top lid and retrieved the pregnancy stick.

"Baby girl," he whispered.

A tidal wave of emotions washed over Derrik's face – shock, disbelief, and finally, an overwhelming joy that lit up his entire being. He pulled Desiree into his arms, laughter bubbling out of him as he spun her around. "Are you serious?"

"Yes! We're having another baby! And I think it might be your princess the way she won't let me keep anything down." Desiree whined.

"Congratulations to the both of you. I was going to tell JuaJua that I thought something was up with you. Those frequent bathroom trips in the morning and even though you're already glowing, you've had the same look I had with the girls," Olivia said with a knowing grin.

Desiree nodded. "Yes ma'am. I told Mommy to please keep it a secret, but I wouldn't've been able to keep it from Derrik after this week. He was starting to notice me getting sick too."

Derrik bobbed his head. "I sure was especially after this morning."

"Congrats, sis," Jayde whispered in Desiree's ear as they embraced.

"Thank you," Desiree replied. She glanced over at Brielle, who was beaming with excitement, clapping her hands enthusiastically.

"Another baby Carter is on the way! I can't wait to plan our princess's shower." Brielle exclaimed, hugging both Desiree and Derrik tightly.

Amid the celebrations, Desiree noticed Justin standing off to the side, looking more nervous than excited. He kept fidgeting with the hem of his sweater and stealing anxious glances toward Brielle when he thought no one was looking. Desiree could see that something was weighing on his mind. "Hey there, are you okay?" she asked quietly as she approached him.

"Huh? Oh uh, yeah, I'm fine," he stammered, avoiding eye contact. "I'm just ... really happy for you guys."

"Thanks, Justin," Desiree said, placing a reassuring hand on his shoulder. "But if there's something bothering you, you can talk to me. You're like part of our family now."

"Really, Desiree, I'm good," he insisted, a tight smile tugging at his lips. But the uncertainty remained in his eyes as they flickered from Desiree and Brielle, who was now chatting animatedly with her own family.

"Okay then," Desiree conceded, giving his shoulder a final squeeze before going back to Derrik's side. I'll let it go for now, but if he doesn't open up soon, I might have to get Derrik involved.

"Baby girl, thank you for this incredible gift. I love you so much." Derrik rasped in her ear as they stood together, watching their family celebrate. "I guess I can tell you this house is going to be perfect to bring our princess next year since it's ours."

Desiree turned around and squealed, "Oh Derrik, I knew it! Daddy, you called it! This house is ours!"

David chuckled and pointed a playful index finger in Derrik's direction, "I told Pumpkin I wouldn't be surprised if you gifted this to her."

"Whatever baby girl wants baby girl is going to get and that's even if she doesn't ask for it."

"Thank you! I love you so much," Desiree hugged him tight, her heart overflowing with joy.

"Alright, everyone!" Justin called out, causing the room to quiet down. "I have an announcement to make, too."

Brielle looked at him, puzzled, as he moved toward her. Her eyes widened with curiosity, as Justin took her hand in his. She barely had time to register what was happening before Justin dropped to one knee, his eyes locked on hers.

"Justin ... w-what are you doing?" Brielle's breath was caught in her throat.

"Everyone who knows me knows that I'm not the best with words," Justin began, his voice shaking ever so slightly. "But I do know this: there is no one more important to me than you, Peaches. And I can't see me doing this thing called life without you by my side."

As he reached into his pocket and pulled out a small velvet box, Brielle's hands flew to her mouth, stifling a gasp. The room fell silent, anticipation hanging thick in the air. Desiree watched from the sidelines, unable to contain her excitement as Justin opened the box to reveal a stunning engagement ring.

"Will you do me the honor of becoming my wife?" Justin asked, his voice choked with emotion.

For a brief moment, time seemed to halt. Tears flooded Brielle's eyes as she stared at Justin's hopeful expression.

"Yes, Justin! A thousand times yes!" Brielle exclaimed, her voice trembling with joy.

As Justin slid the ring onto Brielle's finger, the room erupted into cheers and applause. Desiree smiled as she watched her best friend leap into Justin's arms, their lips meeting in a passionate kiss that spoke volumes about the love they shared.

"Congratulations, you two." Derrik praised.

"Here's to love and family," Desiree added, beaming at the happy couple. She couldn't have asked for a more perfect Christmas morning, surrounded by those dearest to her heart.

As the room buzzed with excited chatter, Derrik leaned in close to Desiree and whispered into her ear, his breath warm against her skin. "You know, even though we already have a baby on the way, I wouldn't mind practicing making one." The deep, velvety timbre of his voice sent a shiver down her spine.

Desiree could feel her cheeks flush as she met his gaze, those dark brown eyes filled with playful desire. "Do you now?" she teased, biting her lip to suppress a smile at the thought of their intimate moments together.

"I can't help but want you more than ever knowing we're creating another miracle together."

Desiree glanced around, ensuring no one was paying attention to the private exchange between them. Everyone was occupied and still basking in the glow of the engagement and pregnancy announcements.

"Okay, let's make our escape."

Derrik grinned, his eyes sparkling with anticipation. "Meet me upstairs in five minutes?"

"Five minutes," Desiree confirmed, stealing a brief, tender kiss from his lips before they parted ways. Derrik slipped out of the room first.

As she climbed the stairs toward their bedroom, Desiree felt a mixture of emotions wash over her: the thrill of their secret rendezvous, the love for her growing family, and the joy of sharing it all with her husband. Without Derrik by her side, she couldn't imagine navigating the complexities of life. He was her anchor and her partner in every way.

CHAPTER 10

From the living room window, Desiree could see that the snowstorm had finally passed. A thick layer of powdery snow now coated the ground outside. It'd taken four days, but the roads leading to their vacation home were now clear of snow and ice, allowing them to leave. The cold outside their vacation home was biting, yet inside it was a cozy oasis.

"Are they gone yet?" Brielle asked.

Desiree peeked back out the window before replying. "Just about. It looks like he just finished getting their stuff packed in the trunk."

"It already feels so much better in here." Brielle threw up a peace sign. "Good riddance!"

With a nod of agreement, Desiree returned her attention to the movements outside. Terrance had just closed the door after securing Janelle inside. While he made his way around the back of the SUV to the other side, Bakari opened the passenger door for Khloe to climb in. For a split second, Khloe twisted her head to look back at the house.

Delusional.

That word immediately popped into Desiree's mind. The longing expression covering her face said it all. Khloe wasn't over Derrik. Her husband had been right in wanting to keep everyone separated. Even though Khloe was in pain, her intentions were clouded in mystery. Nothing about the situation would make sense, but Desiree was happy they were leaving.

Yes. Good riddance!

"Come on, Jayde! You can do this!"

205

Brielle's boisterous voice brought Desiree's attention back to the center of the room to focus on her sister-in-law and everyone else playing Taboo. Jayde's cheeks flushed and she tightly gripped the card in her hand, remaining focused and determined.

"Umm, okay, okay ... I got it! I got it! It's a thing. And-and some people wear it in the winter to keep warm," Jayde hinted, her words rushed.

"A coat!" Brielle yelled.

Jayde shook her head. "No! Umm err ..." She paused for a few seconds.

"Girl, come on!" Brielle clapped her hands. "Time's running out. Give us some words."

"I'm trying, Bri! It's hard not being able to use my hands to show you. Wait! Umm okay I got it! Some people wrap it around their neck!"

"A tie!"

"Ugh, shut up, Uncle Vic! You're loud and wrong. And you ain't even on our team. Dang!" Jayde scolded him in a light-hearted manner.

Juanita shouted, a triumphant smile lighting up her gentle features. "A scarf!"

"Yes! Yes! You got it!" Jayde jumped up and down.

Desiree praised with high-fives. "Great job, Mommy!"

The sounds of Dylan and Dykota's giggles found their way to her ears. They were absorbed in playing with their Christmas toys from their grandparents. Dykota's eyes lit up as he pushed a toy truck across the floor, mimicking engine noises, while Dylan chased after him, clutching a stuffed bear. She glanced over at Derrik, who grinned back at her, his dimpled chin deepening with his smile.

"Alright, alright, my turn!" Vance announced, rubbing his hands together with excitement before he picked up a card.

"Okay Pops hold it down for the fellas. We almost catching up." Derrik cheered, clapping him on the back. Vance winked at him before launching into a series of clues.

"It's in the ocean and people be on it."

"A cruise ship!" Derrik shouted.

His dad waved his hand. "No ... umm, smaller than that. It's like an RV for the seas. You can stay in it if you want."

"Is it a houseboat?" Justin called out.

Vance nodded with a grin. "That man right there's a smart one, Brielle."

"I know Pops. That's my man! Good job, babe!" Brielle hopped up and gave him a quick peck on the lips.

Uncle Vic playfully groaned in annoyance. "Go get a room with all that lovey dovey stuff. Y'all holding up the game." He got up from his spot on the sofa. "Wait, ain't it my turn?"

Olivia threw her hand up in the stop sign gesture. "Nope. It's mine, so go on and sit yourself back down over there."

"Boy, you see how they act when you teach 'em everything," Uncle Vic grumbled, folding his arms across his chest.

Vance retorted, "You ain't teach my wife nothing about this game."

"I know I taught Derrik."

"Nah uhn, must be Jayde. That's why both of y'all stay cheating." Derrik playfully teased her.

Jayde lightly punched Derrik, defending herself. "I do not!"

The banter and joking continued while they played. Uncle Vic kept shouting out answers before anyone else had a chance, and Brielle's competitiveness was almost too much—but this was their family, and Desiree wouldn't replace them for anything.

As the evening rolled in, they gradually transitioned from the game room to settling in the family room around the fireplace. Brielle, Justin, and her parents retreated upstairs to pack as they would be leaving in the morning. Desiree took a deep breath, inhaling the familiar scent of cinnamon-scented candles. The lights from the Christmas tree shone a gentle, gold light throughout the space, creating an intimate setting that invited open conversation. She listened attentively as everyone began to share their experiences from the past week.

Derrik leaned forward, his dark brown eyes reflecting the warmth of the room. "This week it's been a lesson in balancing tradition with adapting to new situations. We can honor the past while still being open to change and growth."

Jayde chimed in, "I've realized how much effort goes into keeping our traditions alive. I used to take it for granted, but now I appreciate all the work that goes into bringing us together, especially during the holidays."

Vance lifted Olivia's hand to his mouth, planting a kiss on the back of it, and then spoke. "This holiday season has shown me that even when things don't go as planned, we can still find joy in our time together. It's not about having a perfect celebration; it's about being present with one another."

"Ya know," Uncle Vic started, his voice softening from its usual boisterous tone, "this year has taught me the importance of cherishing every moment we have together. Not having Athena around for the holidays hits me pretty hard, but being surrounded by all of you makes it a lot easier. I'm proud to say that I have the best family anyone could ask for."

Desiree was inspired by the heartfelt sentiments and words of wisdom the family were expressing as they talked. She realized that what really made the holidays special wasn't in how perfect their traditions had become, but the love and connection that held them all together.

"Surprise family!"

Jordyn was there in the entryway, smiling big. By her side was a tall, handsome young man with dark hair who was helping her in removing her coat as everyone else around the room rose to their feet in shock.

"Sweetheart," Vance said lovingly, placing a hand on her back. "Stop standing there, gawking. Go on. She's really here."

Olivia didn't need any encouragement. She practically sprinted across the living room floor. "Oh, my baby," she whispered as she wrapped her arms around Jordyn, burying her face into her shoulder. "I can't tell you how happy I am to see you."

Jordyn greeted cheerily, "I'm happy to see you too, Ma. Sorry we couldn't make it sooner. We were trying to get here before the snowstorm to surprise everyone."

"Well, better late than never. You've still managed to do just that," Olivia stepped back grabbing hold of her hands, and laughing through her tears. "This is a wonderful surprise."

"Can you believe it?" Derrik whispered in Desiree's ear, his eyes shining with happiness as they watched his parents embrace Jordyn. "This is turning out to be one unforgettable Christmas."

"It really is," Desiree agreed. She got the attention of their twins. "Come on, let's go get some hugs and kisses from Aunt Jordy!"

She and Derrik each took their sons' hands to guide them over to where the rest of the family crowded around Jordyn.

"Jordy, you sneaky thing! You didn't even tell me that you decided to come!" Jayde teasingly chided her.

Jordyn replied, laughing, "I know. I wanted it to be a surprise for you too. There's no way I was gonna miss the holidays with my favorite people."

"Get over here and give me some love, girl." Derrik enveloped his younger sister in a warm hug."

"Hey, big head. Missed you." Jordyn's voice was muffled against his shoulder.

"Missed you more," he admitted, stepping back for Desiree and the boys to greet her.

"Hey, Jordyn," Desiree said softly as she reached out to hug her sister-in-law. "So good to see you."

"You too, sis." Jordyn replied, squeezing her tight. She then pulled away from Desiree to crouch down and greet the twins. "And just look at you two! I swear you've grown an inch since I last saw you!"

Dylan and Dykota smiled before rushing to her, stretching their arms out to be hugged. After the embrace, they took hold of her hands and begged for her to follow.

"Come see what Santa got me!" Dykota pleaded.

Dylan nodded vigorously. "Me too."

Before she could answer, Desiree intervened. "Boys, let Aunt Jordy finish here and then she'll come over. Go, get the toys ready you want to show her."

"Okaaay!" The boys took off running to the other side of the family room where they'd left their toys strewn across the floor.

Desiree saw Derrik staring at his sister's mysterious companion standing beside her. His voice carried a hint of sarcasm as he spoke. "So, you're the infamous boyfriend we've heard nothing about."

"Derrik!" Jordyn gasped in shock and embarrassment.

"Well, you didn't tell me and Desi. Yet, we hear you got a whole boyfriend that Ma and Pops haven't met either."

Desiree playfully mushed her husband's head. "Forgive him. If you have any sisters, you can understand how big brothers are. I have two of my own. Anyway, welcome!"

"Thank you," her boyfriend responded with a grin. "While I don't have any sisters, I'm the youngest of four boys. But Jordy told me to expect her dad and brother to vet me out. I can dig it."

"Long as you know it won't be this one time and we're good with you. What's your name?" Derrik said in a firm tone with his hand out.

"I'm umm, err Nicholas but everybody calls me Nico." The young man took Derrik's outstretched hand, shaking it briefly. His eyes flicked between their dad and him before settling on Vance. "It's great to finally meet all of you."

Vance gave Nicholas a once-over before nodding his approval. He clapped a strong hand on his shoulder, making him wince slightly. "Well, Nico it's about time we got to meet you. Jordy's been keeping you a secret for far too long."

Nicholas peeked at Jordyn and chuckled nervously, rubbing the back of his neck. "I guess she wanted to make sure I was worthy of meeting the family."

"Uh huh," Vance said with a grin. "Well, we'll be the judge of that."

"Where are you from, Nico?" Derrik asked, folding his arms across his chest.

It was obvious Nicholas was doing his best to mask his nerves. He cleared his throat and answered, maintaining eye contact. "Born and raised in Atlanta."

"Interesting," Vance mused. "How do you know Jordyn?"

He didn't have a chance to respond as Derrik hit him with another question. "And what do you do for a living?"

Nicholas coughed nervously and glanced in Jordyn's direction, sharing a moment of understanding. His posture then became strong, and he held his head high, responding with a bold confidence. "We met in our Law and Accounting class at school. I work for my dad at his law firm. I haven't had a big case yet. Just small pro bono stuff right now. My older brothers handle all the bigger cases."

Desiree lips curled into a smile, amused by their dad and Derrik's barrage of questions. Jordyn, on the other hand, was cringing in embarrassment. Impressively, Nicholas gave a composed answer to each query.

"Oh Nico, we didn't catch your last name. Who are you related to? Heh, you never know, we could know your family." Vance said with a chuckle.

Nicholas hit his forehead with the palm of his hand. "How rude of me for not introducing myself properly. I should've mentioned that first." He then proudly announced, "It's Moretti."

Desiree let out a gasp, her head twisting to Derrik whose jaw visibly clenched. Her attention swung to Brielle who'd just entered the room and apparently also caught Nicholas' words. Her eyes were as wide as saucers.

The three of them exclaimed together in shock, "Moretti!"

Mo Flames is an avid reader, writer, wine lover and a superfan of The Office. She pens contemporary romance stories with complex characters, controversial topics, and unpredictable plot twists. Mo's experiences and creativity fuel her written words. She's never been bashful about racy relationship topics. She's unashamed and unapologetically real. It echoes with her tagline, 'leaving that fire between the sheets, literally.'

When she's not writing, she enjoys playing the Sims, reading romance and suspense, binge watching The Office, Snapped, Criminal Minds or any crime television shows. She resides in Atlanta, GA with her husband and daughter.

• • ∽ • •

Make sure you connect with Mo!

https://linktr.ee/moflames
U6[1]

Thank You

From the bottom of our hearts, thank you so much for purchasing a copy of **Holiday Bliss**!

We hope that you have enjoyed reading our Christmas Anthology.

If you have, please make sure to leave a review of this anthology on all your favorite social media websites, so that other readers will find and read **Holiday Bliss** as well.

Here's to you and yours enjoying a most heartfelt (and spicy) Christmas Day - this year and all the ones after!

215

Did you love *Holiday Bliss*? Then you should read *Cupid's Kiss*[1] by K. McCoy et al.!

Are you ready to spend Valentine's Day with us?

Our novel anthology, Cupid's Kiss, features several beloved tropes - including the alpha hero, grumpy/sunshine, and the ever classic soulmates!

Follow these fiery couples along their journey toward finding love - on their own terms.

With Valentine's Day as the theme, each of these six racy stories showcase strong and passionate male leads that are paired with caring and charismatic leading ladies - it's sure to leave you wanting more.

So, grab your sweets and get ready to explore page after page of Cupid's Kiss today!

---

1. https://books2read.com/u/4X0oDg

2. https://books2read.com/u/4X0oDg

Here are the featured authors and their stories for our anthology:

Darie McCoy "Just Kiss Me"

Ryker Stephens was just minding his business, playing blackjack at Anton's, when he laid eyes on a beauty who immediately captured his attention. Love was the last thing on his mind. However, from the moment she walked into his arms, literally, his new mission became providing whatever she needed—and he didn't even know her name yet.

Mo Flames "Make You Mine"

Tanya Ryan is the smart and attractive talent acquisition agent for one of Atlanta's most popular socialites. She can't risk losing her highest paying client lusting after her brother. Yet her client's brother is unwavering in his pursuit to get Tanya to acknowledge their attraction.

Niccoyan Zheng "Venus Next Door"

Isaac Lam likes his quiet, non-festive cul-de-sac just the way it is. Everyone stays to themselves and minds their own business. One visit from his new neighbour Venus 'Vee' Desmond and he senses things are about to change.

J. Nell "Bows and Arrows"

Carys is taken aback when summoned before the council for a special meeting. He is presented with a rare assignment - a mission that, if successful, would alter his life forever.

Latrell R. Morris "The Gentlleman in Red"

Middle school teacher Trina Jackson lives an ordinary life. She comes home, grades papers, watches TV, and repeats it the next day. One evening, she spots a shiny, red sport's car parked in her former neighbor's reserved spot. She's fascinated with the beauty. Unknowingly to Trina, someone's fascinated with her.

K. McCoy "The Continental Honeymoon"

Tasha Daye-Grant couldn't be happier to be Jerome's wife. Until she finds herself unable to voice her unique request to her husband while on their trip overseas.

www.ingramcontent.com/pod-product-compliance
Lightning Source LLC
Chambersburg PA
CBHW020943180626
46814CB00003B/916